WAHIDA CLARK PRESENTS

The Pink Panther Clique

Sunshine Smith-Williams
Jamila T. Davis
Aisha Hall
with
Wahida Clark

Wahida Clark Presents Publishing
60 Evergreen Place
Suite 904A
East Orange, New Jersey 07018
1(866)-910-6920
www.wclarkpublishing.com

Library of Congress Cataloging-In-Publication Data:
Aisha Hall, Sunshine Smith-Williams, Jamila T. Davis
Pink Panther Clique Preview

ISBN 13-digit 978-1936649556 (paperback)
ISBN 13-digit 978-1936649730 (ebook)
ISBN 13-digit: 978-1936649709 (Hardback)
LCCN: 2017904236

1. New York, NY - 2. Money Laundering 3. Hip Hop- 4. African American-Fiction- 5. Music Industry- 6. Federal Prisoners-

Cover design and layout by Nuance Art, LLC
Book design by NuanceArt@aCreativeNuance.com
Cover photo by: Tina Shrivers
Cover model: Stefanie Auree
Edited by Linda Wilson
Proofreader Alanna Boutin

Printed in USA

Dedication

To everyone locked up in the United States and abroad . . .
Keep your head up! We feel your pain.

Prologue

She swallowed a basketball. Her big, pregnant belly protruded, giving off that impression.

"There's no way she should *still* be pregnant. She looks like she's about to drop that load any day now," Sun-Solé, a short, voluptuous, caramel-toned woman with long, straight hair said.

"Shhh. Girl, they're going to hear us. Just keep mopping," Eshe warned. She was a tall, chinky-eyed, brown-skinned girl with a strong New York swagger.

"I can't believe y'all got me down here," Milla said. She was a bright-eyed, almond-toned diva who, even in prison, kept her clothes crisp and her makeup on fleek.

The three women watched from a distance as the pregnant girl wobbled to her seat in the visiting room. They pretended to be cleaning, but they were there for a completely different reason. Sun-Solé was the main one who insisted they volunteer as prison orderlies today, because she could smell drama in the air.

"I'm telling y'all," Sun-Solé said, "I heard Prego on the phone. Baby daddy is coming today. Shit's gonna hit the fan, word to mutha."

Milla rolled her eyes at Sun-Solé. She found it funny to see her prison sister with a mop in her hand because, on the contrary, Sun-Solé was a grown-ass princess. Milla knew how her girl truly lived. Maids and assistants did

1

everything at her home, and she never lifted a finger. Sun-Solé's domestic act had Milla chuckling to herself. Those who only knew her in prison would assume Sun-Solé was a regular Suzy Homemaker who took every cleaning job the prison offered. Anything to get her off the cell block and onto Gossip Street. Sun-Solé cleaned every place from the warden's office to the guards' locker room. Then she'd report all that was going on in the prison to Eshe and Milla. She even knew what was happening in the men's facility. But that was an entirely different story.

Sun-Solé, Eshe, and Milla's eyes were like three sharp surveillance cameras, recording every moment, each of them looking on for various reasons. Sun-Solé was the entertainer. She thought everything was a movie, but instead of it being on the big-screen, she watched things play out in real time. Life was one big reality show to her. She took in the whole scene of Prego with her baby daddy and got high from the action of it all.

Milla watched because she wanted to write about every single injustice that was done to each woman in the prison system. She wanted to tear it down, brick by brick, one story at a time, and end mass incarceration once and for all. She hated the American so-called criminal justice system with a passion because it destroyed families. Specifically, women.

Eshe was extremely unconventional. The female corporate thug, a walking almanac who could probably tell you what the weather was like on any given day in the sixth century. The pragmatic one of the group, Eshe moved when driven by logic only and tried to intervene in situations where she could be of help by adding her opinion. Sometimes, it worked; other times, she had to get a bit ratchet and remind chicks where she was from. Eshe got along with everyone, for the most part, but would buck on the guards at any moment.

All of the ladies were from New York, and they moved with a different swag. They observed Prego on the DL, to see how she would get out of the situation. Prego was just a nickname for the pregnant girl whom they'd been observing. Prego's boyfriend stared her down with a confused look.

"This doesn't feel right. You denied my visits all this time. This shouldn't be the first time I'm seeing you. You won't call me. I'm starting to lose my mind. And look at you; you're as big as a house. This doesn't add up. How can you possibly still be pregnant?"

"You don't understand."

"You've been locked up for ten months and two weeks. You found out you were pregnant before you got here. What the hell is going on? I mean, you need to see a specialist—something! You're going to explode. This shit ain't normal," Prego's boyfriend said.

"There's something I need to tell you." Prego did not look at her man. She stared at the floor as if looking for a quick escape. But there was no escaping reality. At least, not for the ladies in Danbury Federal Prison.

"Well, what is it, baby? It's bad enough you're in here carrying my first child. Is there some type of medical condition I need to know about?" he asked, raising his hands and shaking his head. His perplexed expression caused all three spies to immediately label him as stupid. It didn't matter that he was an attorney. He was a plain ol' dumb ass.

"Visitation is over!" the officer yelled out. "Emergency lockdown. I repeat, visitation is over."

"Awww, shit," one of the spies whispered. "Damn. It's about to go down. Lieutenant Longwood is walking toward them. Look, girl!" Sun-Solé was so excited to see what was about to unfold. Milla was ready to go, and Eshe was in protection mode.

Lieutenant Longwood stepped in front of Prego and her man. "Do you all not hear well? Visitation is over."

"As far as I know, according to policy, visits trump all other prison matters. I'm an attorney. I'm seeing my pregnant fiancée for the first time in months. Can you just give us a minute?" Prego still looked at the floor.

"I don't care what *you* do, but her . . . *She* is going back to her unit, now!" Then he did the unthinkable: he grabbed Prego by her arm and lifted her from her seat. Then he whispered something in her ear. A tear fell from her eye.

"Hey, don't put your hands on her like that. Man, are you crazy?" Prego's baby daddy said. Lieutenant

Longwood released her arm and folded his own arms across his chest.

"You got *one* minute!"

"Baby, does this man do this often? I am going to file a complaint," he said in a low tone.

"Don't bother. I'm stuck here. They do what they want."

"Time's up!" Longwood stated.

"Can I at least give her a kiss? Damn!"

"Hell, no!" he said. "As a matter of fact, Inmate Gaines, don't you have something to tell this clown?"

"Clown? Man, what the fuck is your issue?"

"Not now, Longwood. I'll tell him next time," Prego said.

"Next time? There won't be a next time. You need to let him know, or I will. Today is my last day here, so it needs to be done." She nodded and another tear fell from her eye.

"Okay, I'm gonna just come out and say it."

"Say what?" Baby Daddy asked.

"I'm with Lieutenant Longwood. This is his baby, not yours." Milla, Eshe, and Sun-Solé's mouths dropped open.

"This shit ain't right!" Eshe whispered.

"Well, what the hell are we supposed to do?" Milla added.

"Nothing. What can we do?" Sun-Solé said. By this time, none of them were even pretending to clean. They were just watching. The visiting room was damn near empty, so there was nobody else around to see what was going down.

It was only for a second that they'd looked at each other to speak, but a second was all it took for chaos to break out. By the time they looked back at the love triangle, Baby Daddy was swinging at Lieutenant Longwood. He snuffed the homie.

Crack!

Longwood's jaw fractured. At least that's what it sounded like. Longwood removed his flashlight and caught Baby Daddy in the head. He fell backward. An alarm sounded, and correction officers were every-damn-where. They were pulling Longwood off of Baby Daddy, and another group had pushed the spies to the corner.

Then suddenly there was a piercing cry. "My stomach!" Prego called out. "Oh God! I think my water broke!" The fight was broken up, and medical workers were paged. Milla, Eshe, and Sun-Solé broke through the human barricade of guards who were guarding them in the corner and ran to Prego.

"It's going to be all right," Eshe said, sitting Prego onto the floor.

"No, it's not," she whispered. "This baby ain't neither one of theirs!"

"What! Who's the father?" Eshe asked.

More guards arrived in the visiting room, and they ordered the three spies to get up against the wall so they could be cuffed and taken back to their unit. Sun-Solé was ear hustling. Her hearing was on high alert like a bunny's ears. But nobody heard anything because there was too much noise and chaos. There was blood everywhere from both Lieutenant Longwood and Baby Daddy. Eshe turned around one last time to look at Prego, and she quickly mouthed one name to her. A name they all knew.

Nahhhhh. It can't be! The scandal was deeper than anyone could have ever imagined, and shit was about to hit the fan!

Chapter 1

MILLA

♫ *You the only one I love (uh-huh)/The only man I know that I can trust (yup)/And if I ever should need you, I know you'll come (yeah) ready to kill with a smoking gun (with a smoking gun).* ♫

I sang passionately to Jadakiss's song "Smoking Gun." The words made me think about love and how it used to feel. But at this very moment, the most important thing on my mind was money. I put L. Boogie, Jill Scott, and Adele on rotation to keep me in my zone. Until my office phone rang and interrupted me. After five rings, I picked up. My boss's extension showed on the display in big, black digital numbers.

"Yes, Mr. Darding," I answered.

"Ms. Davison, I need to see you in my office . . . pronto!"

"Sure thing." I hung up and sat there awhile. Although he was my boss, I wasn't the type of employee who asked how high when a higher-up told me to jump. After I was good and ready, I turned my music off and got into professional mode. Professional mode was something that came natural to me, but so did my street persona.

By the way, my name is Jamila Davison, but I go by the name of Milla. I work for Standard American Bank, also known as SAB, one of the largest banks in the country. Currently, I'm a loan agent, and I've got the best track record in our district. I close millions of dollars' worth of loans every single month, and my numbers are steadily increasing. In other words, I'm a beast when it comes to finance. But once I left the office and got into the comfort of my whip, I opened my ashtray, lit up some bud, and blasted Jadakiss. I knew how to turn it on and off. It was a survival mechanism that I'd learned over the years while growing up in Queens. I am who I am, a true black woman who loves her culture. I could pick up a mic and spit a verse with the dudes I grew up with, or I could pick up a mic and sell our bank's latest loan products to a crowd of investors. Because I was equipped with a skill set that allowed me to indulge in the best of both worlds, I was a true chameleon. I grew up not missing a beat in the streets, but also staying on top of my schooling. I was sure my persona would take me far, and I would soon find out just how far once I walked into Mr. Darding's office.

"Ms. Davison. How are you?" he said upon me entering.

"I'm fine. How about you, sir?" I replied, shaking his hand.

"Good, good. Have a seat." I sat my well-rounded booty in the comfort of the black leather chair in front of his desk. He adjusted his seat so he could keep an eye on my legs. And like a salivating dog, he licked his lips as I crossed one leg over the other. *Men. So damn predictable.* It took everything in me to not burst out laughing. Darding was about fifty-five years old, partially bald, with an oversized gut. I didn't give a damn how much money he had; I would never bounce up and down on his lap. Never. Ugh! But still, I smiled, anxious to know what he wanted from me.

"Is everything all right? I see that you wanted me to come here right away. I can't say I'm not nervous. Being called into the principal's office is not always a good thing." He laughed.

"Milla. May I call you Milla?"

"Sure. I prefer it actually. We're all family here at SAB." I threw on the charm, but I wished he would get to the damn point.

"Well, you're here because today is a very special day for you. There's something we noticed about you."

I cleared my throat. "Like what?"

"Most of the clients whom you've been giving loans to are rappers and other famous African Americans. Also, you've been bringing in other individuals who are . . . ummm, let's just say, not the *typical* clients we see come into our bank. Or any bank for that matter." He chuckled at his own joke. I did not. Then I started to think about this impromptu meeting . . . *Awww, shit. If he's going to fire me, he needs to just get to it and stop horsing around. I put a lot of blood, sweat, and tears into this bank. Hell, I brought in new business however I could. So if they're trying to get rid of me, I got a few choice words for his ass!*

So here is the raw truth about how I played the banking game: I just happened to see an opportunity with these celebrities and wanted to help them while helping myself. I had to pull teeth sometimes to get them approved for loans. I even had to tell little white lies sometimes because a lot of them didn't have tax returns or had cash businesses. But what I did was still good. Helping guys with new record deals get their first Bentley, Maybach, Rolls-Royce, or Lamborghini. Taking dope boys from the projects to gated communities. So what, I made up pay stubs. They paid their bills, and that was all that mattered. I was making the bank lots of money because all my people paid their loans back. They better had, or else they would have to deal with me personally. I figured I would sell myself before he gave me the bad news. You know, try to save face.

"I just spoke with Jadakiss. He's a famous rapper right here in New York, and he was approved for a $2 million mortgage not too long ago. I got him to put a million down, so he's well invested. I can tell you, I know him personally, and he will not only pay, but pay early. And Zab Judah, five-time champion boxer, he just paid off a $3.5 million loan that I worked very hard to get for him. I know my methods were a little nontraditional, but my goal is to make this bank #1 in the world. The world, sir. No other bank could do it, but I got it done. If there is something wrong with the—" He interrupted me.

"No, there is nothing wrong. Actually, we think what you're doing is great. You're bringing in some unusual characters, yes, and it's making the bank a lot of money. There is some good news that recently came down the pipeline." He leaned in closer from his side of the desk. "We want to promote you. We want you to bring more of your, uh, your people into our establishment. It's a win-win situation for all of us." He got up and closed his office door, then sat back down and talked in a hushed tone.

"I know a lot of these rapper characters don't have good credit, Milla. We also noticed you seem to know a lot of . . ."—now he went into an all-out whisper—"drug dealers and street guys. But they still have plenty of money, and we can still sell houses to these people. We just need you and your wit to help continue to bridge that gap. We'll give you whatever you need. There is just one condition."

"Okay . . . and what's that?" His breath stank of the rotten bullshit that was about to fly out of his mouth any second. *Here it comes.*

"Well, all of these types of loans need to start with 14 percent interest."

"Fourteen percent?" I repeated, shocked. I looked at him as if he'd passed me the whip and asked me to beat his slaves for him. He'd lost his mind. My stare lingered. *He can't be serious. That amount is outrageous!* I was about to get up and walk out, but I pondered his offer briefly. Yeah, he thought he was getting over by exploiting my people, giving them high interest loans that any knowledgeable person would never pay. However, I saw an opportunity to help a lot of people, and my brain had already started churning out a plan to get around that interest rate crap. I could work my magic once I got an opportunity to get creative. And it sounded like he was giving me that power.

"What exactly would the position be?"

"Special accounts manager."

"And the meaning of *special*?" I asked, raising a freshly waxed eyebrow.

"Well, we'll leave that to you. We can get creative. But, of course, we want the bank to be known for bridging the gap and giving minorities opportunities that no other bank has done. And the best part of it is: we'll give you your own team with underwriting power to approve loans up to $5 million! We've got about $500 million to lend. Who knows, you can be the Oprah Winfrey savior for your people. Think about what you can do. Not just for yourself, but for your community." Never in America does a bank suddenly tell a black person they have access to so much money, to give to more black folks. *Something is off with this. This is corporate America, and we aren't welcome here.*

"Of course, I'll accept. I love it! Thank you so much for the opportunity, Mr. Darding." We shook on it. My name was already ringing bells. I surely didn't want to sound off any alarms. If I felt that he was up to something crazy, I would back out. But I'd wait until that happened, if ever.

I exited the bank, jumped in my Benz, and celebrated with a fat-ass blunt. Yeah, Milla Winfrey had a crazy ring to it! But I also found out that if something sounded too good to be true . . . it usually was!

Chapter 2

SUNNY-SOLÉ

My momma named me Sunshine-Solé because she knew I would shine. And I do—like a D color diamond sparkling in the sun. Maybe she should've just named me Diamond since I wore so many of them. That's probably why the prosecutor kept glancing back at me. I shouldn't have worn my wedding ring set. Every time I raised my hand, I'm sure I blinded the judge and prosecutor because they both were acting as if they couldn't see the scandal unfolding right before their eyes. Shit, no disrespect, but Ray Charles could even see this bullshit. You see, my husband and I had always been getting money. We had so many legitimate businesses, that all of our street money got washed flawlessly. There was no proof that we moved a few bricks, printed a few thousand pounds of counterfeit money, and worked out a fair deal with the Italian mob to run our businesses in their territory. The illegal dealings are only a small part of our major operations. One would never know what we were doing, but the Feds insisted on sniffing and digging until their hunger got the best of them, and they went in for the kill.

About three months ago, I had finally had the house to myself. I'll never forget it. While relaxing in my master suite Jacuzzi, I was skimming through the DuPont registry and scoping out that new Bentley Bentayga and listening to CNN. My alarm system went off, followed by a call from the security company. There was no knock and enter. No warning. They just broke the door down and shouted, "We've got a warrant!" My breath left my body as I stood naked in the water with my mouth hanging open. I stepped out of the tub as fast as I could and grabbed my La Perla edenic silk robe from the heated rack. It was as warm as a freshly baked loaf of bread, but the goose bumps appeared as though I was bare in the middle of Antarctica.

"Who's in my crib?" I screamed, as if my life was in danger. Before I could walk out of the bathroom, ten or so FBI agents swarmed in front of me.

"Ma'am, you need to get dressed and come with us," an agent said.

"Do you have a warrant?" I asked. One of them flashed it in my face so fast I could barely read it.

"Now, like I said . . . get dressed."

"Where the fuck is my copy?" I asked, grilling him. The left corner of my top lip rose. He ignored my question and my frown.

"You need to put on something decent." Damn, it was uncomfortable the way his blue eyes roamed from my head down to my toes.

"I would, if you get the hell out. Get out of my bathroom, and I'll get dressed."

"We can't let you out of our sight."

"Then it looks like we have a problem."

"Looks that way," the smart-mouthed one said, smirking. I smiled back.

"What's your name?"

"Special Agent Jackson, and this is my team." I nodded but never took my eyes off him.

I calmly spoke, "Suri, activate security cameras. Activate vocal record. Male FBI agents are standing in my bathroom trying to force me to undress in their presence while . . ."

He threw his hand up in defeat and rolled his eyes. And I crossed my arms.

"Somebody get a female agent up here," he said, cutting me off. "Come on, guys, step out. Search the bedroom. And be thorough!"

They didn't find anything but money. A whole lot of it. About a million dollars. But what they reported finding was $100,000. They stole the rest. They charged my husband, H, with money laundering, but they couldn't connect anything to me. He is currently on trial, but it seems he'll be going home. You see, when you live the way we do, you always have security cameras. The footage showed them going into our stash room and piling money into duffle bags. It clearly showed much more than $100,000. With that evidence, there should be no problem with my husband getting vindicated. I couldn't wait for the jury to see those crooked muthafuckas getting busted stealing our money. The case had to get tossed.

My husband's lawyer got up to speak. My king turned and winked at me. I gave him a head nod and blew him a kiss.

"And now, Your Honor, the defense would like to present to you our most crucial piece of evidence yet—the security footage from the Williamson family home." The video began to play on the big screen. It clearly showed them taking money, but then the video suddenly turned off.

"Your Honor," said the court technician, "we seem to have experienced some type of glitch that corrupted the file."

"Fix it!" Mr. Caltron, my husband's attorney said. "Fix it!" They tried for the next half hour, and then broke for recess. When court resumed, the file had been totally corrupted, and they claimed there were no copies. I could not contain myself.

"This is bullshit! Y'all not playing fair!" I stood up and shouted. "This is unacceptable. They just don't want to be exposed. Those agents are all dirty. All of 'em!" The judge, Brenda Doom, could have called a mistrial. Something. Anything! But instead, she called it an "unfortunate event." And she said the trial would continue. This was unheard of. The one thing that could prove our case was no longer available. Was this shit even legal? I didn't know what to do. So I walked toward the judge.

"Mrs. Williamson, you may want to calm down before I hold you in contempt of court."

"I don't give a shit! A black man can't get a fair trial in this country. This is outrageous!" The marshals intervened and literally dragged me out of the courtroom. They told me to leave, or I would be arrested. I was beside myself with anger. I was so hot tempered. I felt like the Phoenix. They deaded my king and me on our bread, and they were trying to cover it up. Actually, they weren't *trying* to cover it up . . . They'd already done it! I felt violated. But if it was the last thing I ever did, I would get to the bottom of this and expose these "corrupted-ass suits" one way or another.

Enough was enough!

Chapter 3

ESHE

Did I forget something? I thought as I arrived at my office early. Puzzled, I pulled up in a customized black Range Rover, followed by two black Escalades. Each one was driven by two of the most loyal men I had in my life, Marcellus and Jeremy. They both worked for me, but they were more like my brothers. Jeremy, who went by the nickname Jerry, stepped out of his truck first, rocking a Tom Ford suit. He walked over to my truck and opened my door. A light drizzle fell, so he held an umbrella for me. I held onto his arm. And when Marcellus exited his truck, the three of us entered the building. They both would protect me with their lives, and their loyalty was priceless.

Marcellus used to work for a luxury car dealership. I knew he was a lyrical beast with great potential when I saw him moving cars to dope boys who didn't have an ounce of credit. Jeremy was a kingpin in the dope game. He barely missed an indictment, but witnessing how thorough he ran his organization, I knew he'd be a good corporate thug. He brought a different energy to the office environment. Everybody respected them. I entrusted them to run the company in my absence.

We all went into our private offices to get to work. We traded gold, oil, natural gas, diamonds, rubber, and pretty much anything that sold on the international market that was worth millions and in large amounts. I was anxious to check what my bank roll was hittin' like since I closed a pretty good deal a few days ago. This morning was payday, and that always got me excited. I pulled up my account online, and my smile flipped into a frown. I didn't like what I was seeing. No deposits today.

The balance was exactly the same, $9,659,000.19. I was sitting on seven digits, but I went to bed last night expecting to wake up sitting on eight. I called my client to find out what was going on and why my money hadn't transferred over yet. I expected to see another $500,000. He answered on the first ring.

"Kev, what's up? Did something happen at the trade desk that I need to know about? Why didn't the deal close?"

"Yeah, something happened all right! Some bullshit! They're telling me I can't trade, and my application is denied." I slammed my fist on the desk and bit my bottom lip.

"What do you mean you can't trade? Why did they deny your application?" I asked my potential client. His name is Kevin James, a young black man who owns a small gas station in North Carolina.

"Because, well, they said I don't have enough assets."

"I'm looking at your bank statement right now. You're the CEO of a company worth over ten million. You're only trading with less than a million. You have more than enough money. What the hell are they talking about?"

"No, the oil company will only deal with someone worth $100 million or more. I'm nowhere near that valuation. I just got the new trade instructions today. Looks like I'm out. Even though I'm only spending less than 10 percent of that, they've made the requirements impossible."

"That doesn't make any sense. It's the stupidest rule I've ever heard of. Okay, Kevin, let me find out what's going on, and I'll call you back. I'll figure something out." I ended the call and immediately announced to my staff that we were having a meeting. They piled into my office.

"Hey, guys," I said to the eight of them. "We've got some serious work to do. We've been setting up trades for folks for months now. We've introduced more African Americans to the world of commodity trading than any other company. We've made many of our brothers and sisters rich beyond their dreams. Thanks to you guys, we've done some beautiful things together. But there is another side to this. Something I do not like. I've noticed now that since more minorities are getting involved in these types of deals, the requirements have gotten damn near impossible. They're pushing us out. And you guys know me . . . I am not going to let that happen. So here's the deal: anyone who calls us looking for assistance in qualifying for a trade deal, put 'em through to me. If the deal closes, you get 15 percent automatically!" I raised the commission by 5 percent. We were used to closing deals that hit around $500,000, so my employees easily saw $50,000 checks on a weekly basis.

"Sounds good to me," Marcellus said, rubbing his hands together.

"Me too," added Jerry, who was in charge of marketing, and he also had another job . . . my enforcer. When someone owed us money or didn't pay, Jerry had a way of making sure they made good on their promises. "I need to holler at you, though," Jerry said when the meeting was over. "In private," he whispered.

I got up from my very comfortable seat and dismissed everyone except Marcellus and Jerry.

"What's on your mind, bro?" I asked.

"We've got a problem," Jerry said.

"A serious one," said Marcellus. I sat back down.

"Tell me!" I closed my eyes briefly, not knowing what to expect.

Jerry nodded to the side, indicating for me to follow him. Once again I was out of my seat. We got on the elevator and headed down to the basement of the thirty-five-story building.

"Why are we down here?" I asked. All I could hear was the click-clacking of my Giuseppe heels against the concrete floor. Neither of my brothers spoke. We turned a corner, and they eyed one another. They lifted what looked like an oversized trash can, and I jumped back, grabbing my chest. The body of a middle-aged white man wearing a very straight cut Canali suit lay inside.

"Boss Lady . . ." Marcellus tried to say something. I shook my head.

"Close that shit," I said, disgusted.

"Eshe, I caught him in the office last night. I came back here after I realized I left my wallet. It was about midnight, and I caught him trying to plant some dope in your office," Jerry said.

"What the hell!"

"He had a gun. So I didn't think twice; I hit 'im in the head immediately."

"Jerry, why didn't you call me?"

"I didn't want to ruin your trip. I knew you'd be back this morning. After I searched him, I found this . . ." Jerry showed me a badge. The man was a U.S. Secret Service agent.

Awwww, fuck!

Chapter 4

MILLA

Milla Winfrey has a nice ring to it. My coworkers had a money clip with MILLA WINFREY engraved on both sides. It was their way of acknowledging my hard work. I hustled like Oprah. A diamond stud sat perfectly in the middle. Cute. And I definitely kept it full of them big-face Benjamins. I left the office and headed over to Hit Makers, the studio in Harlem where so many hip-hop hits were made. I'd just got a call from Cedrick Williams, CEO of Platinum Records.

When I got inside, there were so many chicks walking around in skimpy clothing; it looked like they were auditioning for a video. For a moment I thought I was on a set. Studio groupies. Most of them were broke, trying to find a man to pay their rent. I had the opportunity to use my goodies to come up, but I found that using my brain led to better opportunities and monetary stability. That's what I was about . . . being comfortable. I could write checks and never worry if they would clear. This new position gave me a lot of power. And I planned to use it.

"So what's up, Cedrick?" I asked as I walked into the engineer's room in the second-largest recording room, known as Studio C. Jadakiss was in the next room over,

Studio B. Cedrick smiled, and then nodded. He continued to bop his head to the music as his newest artist, King-G, also known as KG, laid down a track that was definitely going to be a hit. He was a beast. He had about seven mix-tapes out and was without a deal. Everybody wanted to sign him, and so did Cedrick.

"Annnnd . . . That's a wrap!" The producer cut the track, and King-G took his headphones off. He then walked out of the booth and gave Cedrick and the producer a pound. The producer bounced, leaving just the three of us.

KG was very handsome. He was about six foot two, covered in tattoos, and caramel toned. He kept himself in shape—fine was an understatement. But I'd seen many of his type, and they all were interested in the same type of girls: THOTS. So I didn't even bother taking a third look.

"King-G, this is Milla Davison. If you don't mind waiting for me over in the studio with Jay, I'll be there to holler at you."

"That's cool. Nice to meet you, pretty," King-G said. I smiled. He exited the room.

"So what you need, Big Ced?" I asked. He began talking in a hushed tone.

"Listen, I'm just gonna keep it straight with you. Platinum Records is about to go bankrupt. We signed two other mix-tape artists and thought we had stars. Their singles went crazy. But both albums flopped. We lost $20 million between the two of them. It really put us in a bind. I know King-G can get us out of this slump. He's a star. Just listen to this." He then began playing a few cuts. His music was like nothing I'd ever heard. He was most definitely going to be the next big thing. I liked Cedrick; he was a gambler and a risk taker. I respected that because it took risks to reap rewards. Nobody knew that better than me.

"That's dope. Sounds good. So what do you want from me?" I wanted to get to the point of this meeting. He said it was urgent.

"I want to sign him. But I don't have the money to give him the type of signing bonus that these other labels are offering. So I wanted to know if you can help me borrow the money." He twisted his head in one of those "I'm not so sure" gestures.

"How much we talkin'?" I asked.

"Maybe $3 million!"

"Three mill? That's gonna be tough if your assets are strapped."

"Come on, Milla. You're the only person I know that can make this happen. Everybody knows you're the go-to lady."

"Let me think about it, and I'll get back to you. I'll see what I can do."

"That's what I'm talkin' 'bout. I'll even obligate some of the record sales royalties to go toward directly paying the loan back."

"As long as your artist knows that's what you're doing. I don't wanna be a part of any artists getting duped by their label. We go back a long way, so, of course, I am going to try to look out. But the loan needs to be the label's obligation, not the artist's."

"I'm fine with that, Milla."

"A'ight. I'll have the lawyers draw everything up and make sure we're good."

"That's my girl."

"But you know, I'll need a little something to get started because I have to make certain arrangements. I'll also need all of your financials."

"I'll e-mail everything over to you."

"No, mail it to me at this address." I then handed him a card. I didn't need a paper trail, just in case I had to get unorthodox.

We exited the studio to meet up with King-G. He was kicking it with Jadakiss. Jada was so impressed that he decided to hop on a track with KG last minute. TI happened to walk in the studio, and he listened as well. When they were done, they looked at Cedrick. TI nodded and said, "If you don't sign him, I will." Jadakiss agreed. And when Jada put his seal on a young cat, he had to be fresh. And King-G definitely was certified. I could understand why Cedrick wanted him so bad.

Cedrick went off with Jadakiss to kick it for a little while, and I was left all alone with KG.

"I'm starving," he said. "I been thuggin' it out in the studio for two days straight. A nicca needs to eat. I'm worn out and exhausted," he said, throwing back a bottle of water.

"I bet. But your hard work is paying off. Your music is on point. You've got a lot of talent. You're making hits."

"Somewhat. I'm just waiting for the right deal to come along. I got a lot of things in my life that aren't quite right yet, feel me? I'm waiting for the right hit to come to me, the right label, the right lady . . ." he said, eyeing me. Something about the way he said it created a moment of silence. Okay, I saw his game. It was cute, but he was an unsigned artist who couldn't do anything for me right now. The man who I chose to give my time and energy to would have to be already established. Been there and done that with those on the cusp of success. I wasn't into gambling anymore. I needed a little bit more this go-round.

"I hear you. Well, the only advice I can give you is to keep looking. I'm sure if you have patience, all of those things will eventually come along."

"Yeah, it most definitely will, ma." He smiled. And then he did that thing with his eyes again. I looked the other way. Just when things were getting a little awkward, Cedrick came back into the room. He nodded for us to follow him, and we both did.

The three of us went to the office in the back of the building. Cedrick was smiling and sweating at the same time. What was he up to? Finally, I heard it, and I shouldn't have been surprised, but I was. Cedrick offered King-G a deal with a $7 million signing bonus. I froze. My eyes widened as I processed what he just said! *What the hell is he doing? I haven't even gotten a green light on the deal. There isn't a written contract, written proposal, or one financial document in my possession.* And the pressure was now on, because if Cedrick couldn't make good on his word, his career would be done. I smiled and tried to act happy, but I was really looking at him like he had lost his damn mind. Had I been psychic, I would have known that this deal was the worst possible thing I could have ever done in my life!

Chapter 5

SUNNY-SOLÉ

With my game face on, I calmly sat in the governor of New York's oversized plush office. I made a few phone calls and fronted like I was a member of his New York campaign team. He owed me a favor, but he didn't know it yet. He was one of my few customers I dealt with in my underground world. He purchased some counterfeit bills to replace some of the taxpayers' money he stole from the MALCOLM AND MARTIN MAKE A CHANGE FUND. Money that was supposed to be used to help promote minority business opportunities. Because many blacks didn't know about the fund, it was easy to exploit. And his crooked ass took $1.3 million from it last year. I wasn't stupid. I kept track of each and every person who entered my hidden world. Initially, I found people who were in desperate situations and needed money. My way of helping them out was by providing fake bills. After a while, I earned a reputation for having the best "authentic-looking" fake money, and that's why certain people with money problems sought me out. To protect myself, I hired a runner to screen all potential customers. Through him, I found out I had a potential customer coming down from Albany who wanted a large amount of money as soon as possible. The person checked out; they weren't law enforcement, but it was close.

The place where they wanted to meet my runner was at some mansion in New Rochelle. It was owned by a corporation, owned by another corporation, owned by another. My curiosity was piqued. So I did some digging. And when I found out who *really* owned that property, I was floored.

A man named Cliff Barnes met with my runner. Turns out, he was the silent business partner of the most powerful man in New York.

The governor!

I wouldn't have believed it had I not seen it with my own eyes. When I found out that the person who made the purchase was strongly connected to him, I followed them the day the drop was made and saw him hand Governor Wyzask the package of counterfeit bills. I snapped a picture of the exchange, and I now had my evidence, which I planned to use to my advantage. If he didn't want to be exposed, he needed to cooperate. And that was easy. All he had to do was sit and listen to what I had to say.

"How can I help you, Mrs. Williamson?" the governor asked as he walked in. He sat down and gave me a fake smile. "You must know some powerful people, if you were able to get a meeting with me on such short notice."

"I know who I need to know." My face was still and stoic. I wanted him to know I meant business.

"Have we met before?" he asked.

"Not exactly. Let's just say we've done business together."

"I'm not really sure what you mean by that. What kind of business? Personal or for the good people of New York?" He smiled. This muh'fucka didn't have a clue what I had over his head. But he was about to find out.

"Let me be straight with you, *Governor* . . . I drove all the way here to Albany because I have an issue that only you can resolve. I'd like to show you something."

"All right," he said slowly. His tone was curious, and he loosened his tie.

"I'd like a pardon for my husband. He's in federal prison right now, but—" The governor put his hand up and shook his head.

"Okay, let me stop you right there. First and foremost, I have no idea who your husband is and why you're really here. Second, if he's in federal prison, I cannot help you. I deal with matters of New York State only. Sorry you came all the way here, ma'am, but he needs to file a commutation pardon request with the president."

"Actually, I have a better idea. He needs to be charged with a state crime. He'll be summonsed to leave on a writ to deal with the pending charges you created. Then he will be moved to a New York State prison. After that, he'll get pardoned . . . by you. Then, I will board a private jet and leave this country with my husband and son." He looked at me as though I asked him to marry his own mother.

"Get out! I'm calling the police. How dare you come in here with this insanity!" He picked up the phone.

"Put the phone down, motherfucker," I said as I crossed my legs. "If you're calling them, tell them to pick your crooked ass up as well. I know what you've been doing." He placed the black office phone back on the receiver.

"What are you talking about?"

I turned my phone's screen in his direction and played a video. It showed him taking the package that I knew had the money in it. Counterfeit money.

"You know *exactly* what I'm talking about, Governor, sir. You see, this video I have is proof that you are the true recipient of $1,300,000 of false money. Counterfeit. Fake. Falsely printed bills. I think you understand! You purchased them for $300,000, and, as a matter of fact, you have another order pending. Does *that* refresh your memory?" I didn't give him a chance to even respond. I kept on talking. "You stole the money from a fund for black people. You just figured nobody would find out. Turns out, I do a thorough check on every customer I deal with. So like I said, you'll be calling the district attorney out of Queens and charging my husband with something. I'll let you pick the charge. And then you *will* pardon him. You're up for reelection this year. I'd hate for this information to get out and go public. Or even get to the FBI."

I could see the steam coming from his head, and I sensed fear. I knew I had him in my pocket, and he'd do anything to keep from being exposed.

"Are you done?" he asked with his face screwed up.

"Actually, no. One more thing . . . I want a meeting with crooked-ass Judge Brenda Doom. She's federal."

"I can't guarantee you that."

"Oh yes, you can. Not only are you *going* to guarantee it, but you're going to *set it up!*" I'd never blackmailed anyone in my life, but I had to do something. I couldn't let my husband go down in a crooked-ass justice system, where everybody who handed out justice was crooked as well! I had my king on my back and my son on my shoulders, and I'd be damned if I allowed this bullshit to split up my family!

Chapter 6

ESHE

Agent Perrell. That was his name. We were on our way to get rid of the body. We removed his clothing, destroyed his phones and all other communication devices we found on him, and prayed that once we dumped him, his body would never be discovered. Anything that might have been being tracked showing his location was smashed to pieces. I went with them to the Osmogos River to dump the body because if anything went down, I would not let my brothers take responsibility for it. Jerry shot him. And Marcellus and I were going to help finish everything off. We were in this as a family. Point-blank!

We opened the trunk of the rental, and my brothers pulled the body out. Marcellus lifted the body and dropped him on the ground. "Uggh, mmm." There was a groan. The low fog and moist ground added to the eerie feeling.

"What the hell was that?" I asked. It took a second, but after locking eyes with one another, we all looked down in the direction of where the noise was coming from. The ground. And sure enough, the body moved a little.

"Impossible!" Marcellus said.

"He's not dead? You've gotta be kidding me. This can't be possible. Fuck!"

Jerry pulled his piece out. "I'll take care of it." He aimed it at the agent's head. He moaned again. Shit. This wasn't supposed to be happening this way.

I stepped over him, sheltering his body with mine. "No! Don't shoot him!" I knew that if I had just said it, Jerry might have pulled the trigger anyway. I had to make sure he didn't.

"Boss Lady, we have to make sure he's dead," Marcellus warned.

"He survived a gunshot wound to the head. He wasn't meant to die. We can't."

"Nah. Eshe, you're trippin'. We let him live, and then what? He's gotta go." Then suddenly I felt something on my leg. I looked down, and it was the agent's hand wrapped around my ankle. His eyes were fluttering.

"Pluh-pluh-please. Don't. Duhh . . ." He couldn't finish speaking. He was in and out of consciousness. But he was breathing.

"My final answer is no. Cellus, get him in the backseat. And be careful moving him."

"You're making a big mistake, Eshe. We'll do life in prison," Marcellus added. My mind was made up. "This is a Secret Serv—"

"You think I don't know that?" I said, frustrated.

"You acting like we—" I interrupted him with my body language. I threw up my hand and shook my head to signal that I didn't want to talk.

"Whatever!" Marcellus said, kicking the dirt. He hated when I did that. But I needed to think.

"You know how she gets when she's going into problem-solving mode," Jerry said to Marcellus. He nodded, knowing that I was plagued with the decision to do the right thing *and* protect my brothers at the same time. I wasn't a killer. I didn't like ending life at all. Had he been dead, fine. We could have dealt with that. But seeing a person clinging to life was something I'd never seen before, and I didn't have the heart to kill a begging man. Jerry drove, and I rode shotgun. Marcellus got in the back with the butt naked white agent. His chest was moving up and down. He was alive, but barely.

I pulled out my phone and made a call.

"Dende! Cuz, how are you?"

"I'm good. I'm shocked you have spare time to call your favorite cousin."

"I know. I have got to do better. But, cuz, I've got an emergency situation that only you can help me with."

"You okay?" he asked, truly concerned.

"Not really, Dende. I need your help ASAP."

"Okay, what's up? I've got a scheduled surgery in two hours."

"Can we talk face-to-face, in private?"

"Of course. Sure. Anything for you, Eshe."

"This is life or death, Dende. I'm coming right now."

"Hurry, Eshe. I can't be late for surgery. You know the hospital."

"Absolutely. I'm on my way."

My cousin Dende was a general surgeon. I met him at the hospital, and told him how dire the circumstances were for the agent. I offered him a hundred grand to see the Secret Service agent privately and to make sure he stayed alive. Dende hesitated at first, but when he heard the seriousness and urgency of my tone, he agreed. Thank goodness for Dr. Dende Hunt. He snuck him in and took him straight to the basement of the hospital, right behind the medical records office. He said nobody came back there. Dende set up a bed, hooked him up to all types of equipment that he snuck down, and he immediately began working on the agent. Jerry stood watch to make sure nobody came into the room. If so, he'd distract them.

"I can lose my job for this. My license," Dende stated.

"I know, cuz. I know. But I could lose my life if you don't help us. I'll pay off all your medical school bills. Anything you need."

He looked at me. "All of them?"

"Yes, and some. Just don't let this man die. I'll explain later."

"I hope you're not into anything crazy," he said as he injected the man with what I assumed was some type of anesthesia. "The bullet must have passed through. That's a good sign. I think he'll survive." I turned and looked at Marcellus. We both knew the problem with what my cousin just said. If the bullet passed through, that meant it was still possibly in the office. We had to get back there and handle our business. I left Jerry with my cousin. Marcellus and I headed back to the office.

We cleaned wherever we saw blood. I immediately had someone go to Home Depot and get new carpet and a crew to install it. I wanted the old shit up in less than an hour and the new carpet laid down before any of my employees had the chance to arrive at work. We had four hours to replace everything and find the bullet and shell casing.

By 8:15 a.m., everything was done. If I could have, I would have given everyone the day off, but I couldn't. We were holding tens of millions of dollars of our clients' money, and we could not be unavailable at any time during normal business hours. That wasn't the way this worked. My phone rang. It was my cousin Dende.

"He'll live. He's recovering. But he's gotta be out of here in the next two hours. I'll get him set up wherever you want him to rest. Then I'm done, cuz. You're on your own."

"Thank you! Thank you so much, Dende." I called Jerry and told him to take the man to the Westin Hotel. Dende could set him up there. I had to find out why this man had done what he did. And I knew he wasn't acting alone.

My employees arrived by 8:30. I tried my best to hide the stressed look on my face. I sat behind my desk, tapping my favorite pen on the imported ebony wood. I spent more time here than in my own home. The phone rang, distracting me. It was my client, Mr. Kevin James.

"Hello, Kevin," I said.

"Any news?" he asked.

"Mr. James, give me ten minutes, and I'll call you right back." I hung up the phone. I pulled up his file and looked over his assets. The oil trader was wrong for denying him. One hundred million dollars was way too much money to expect him to have. They were keeping wealth among the same types of people, and pushing everyone else who didn't look like them out. I'd already been dealing with one crisis, and I didn't know what the future held. So I decided, fuck it. What did I have to lose? I was going to take a huge risk, unlike one that I'd ever taken before. I added an extra zero to his account balance and put my stamp of verification on it. I wasn't going to let something so stupid stop a good man from reaching another level. He was now worth over $100 million on paper.

I called him and told him what I had done. I took care of his banker, who would verify it if the oil company wanted to confirm his balance. I explained to him that it was totally his choice, and my fee would remain the same. He agreed. I was tired of seeing my people always get the bad end of the deal. So I did what was necessary. I ended the call with Mr. James when Marcellus knocked on my door.

"Boss, we got a problem. The Secret Service is up front, and they're asking to talk to you."

This *was* a problem. We never found the bullet or the casing!

Chapter 7

MILLA

I worked my magic with the underwriters and got it done. I got the $12 million loan approved for Cedrick. Around the office they really started calling me Milla "Winfrey" because they said I handled them checks like Oprah. They thought it was a nice compliment. I took it as something to aspire to. I couldn't wait to share the news with him. Plus, it would get him off my back. He'd been blowing up my phone nonstop because he needed that money. It only took me about three weeks to get the check cut. And I was meeting with him today to go over the terms. Terms that I would explain he could not deviate from, no matter the circumstances.

If he did not hold up his end of the bargain, the loan would default. A defaulted loan in an amount so high would lead to an account probe. An account probe would then lead to an investigation. And that was not something I was going to allow to happen. So before I placed these checks in his possession, I needed to see his master plan. Every detail of it. There were two checks. One for four million, which would be given to King-G, and another for eight million, which was made out to him to help save his label.

Cedrick was on point. His attorneys were present, and he'd laid out the plan for repaying the money. I felt confident handing over the check. He seemed to have his repayment plan together, and I knew his reputation as one of the top record label owners was important to him. He didn't want his legacy to be that of another failed giant in the hip-hop industry. He had a point to prove. And because of that, I knew he would make good on his promise. Our loan agreement was confidential. Nobody knew that Cedrick borrowed that money. But I was there for support and to make sure that he did what he was supposed to do. KG only knew me as Cedrick's banker. That was all he needed to know.

He hadn't signed the contact yet, but as soon as we left this meeting, we headed over to Platinum Records headquarters to meet up with him. When we walked in, the place was buzzing. All the label employees, A&Rs, and execs were standing around with champagne bottles and confetti, ready to celebrate once the deal was done. As KG entered the building, everybody watched him walk into the boardroom with his attorneys. He had a whole damn team. I was surprised he could afford that. Most new artists could barely pay their bills, but he impressed me with his interest in protecting his future. Smart. I must say, him in a suit was a sight to see. KG was so handsome, he had what I called the "stare-effect"—where you had to check yourself for looking so hard, and then turn the other way. His

When he sat down, I cleared my throat. He looked at me and smiled. I smiled back and quickly turned away. His lawyers explained that they reviewed the record deal, and it looked standard; they only had a few changes to make regarding concert and tour proceeds. They hashed that out in about fifteen minutes, and then it was time to sign. KG inked his signature, and so did Cedrick. They shook hands, and the check was exchanged.

I watched King-G, the man with the stare-effect swag. He just got four million, and his expression did not change one bit. What was up with this dude? Nobody in the world was that smooth. He passed the check over to his lawyer and got up to leave. When he stepped outside of the conference room, the building went berserk. They popped bottles and cheered. I was happy for him.

After I shook hands with Cedrick, congratulating him for signing such a promising artist, I started toward the elevators.

"Hold that door, ma," KG said. He got on the elevator with me, and when his lawyers tried to get on, he told them to catch the next one.

"That was rude!" I said, jokingly.

"I've seen enough of them cats for one day. I wanted to invite you to my party tonight."

"Party? Oh, thanks, but I don't party like that. I've got too much work to do." I didn't know what the hell I was saying; my mouth was moving on its own without much thought or guidance behind the words that were spilling out.

"Word? That's how you feel? I don't just want you to come to the party. I want you to be my date for the night." I almost dropped my Chanel bag.

"Your date?" I laughed.

"Yeah, is that an issue? You got somebody in your life that would have a problem with that?"

"I mean, not really. But you don't even know me."

"I know you're swaggy with it. You get to your bag. Intelligent. What else I need to know? I just wanna chop it up with you, if you don't mind," KG said.

"Okay, let me think about it. It's early. I'll call you and tell you if I decide to go . . . around eight tonight." Just then the elevator door opened, and I walked off so fast I left smoke in my trail. "Congratulations," I said, before walking off. He stood there and watched me for a minute, and then yelled in my direction.

"Ay, yo! Hold up, Milla! How you gon' say you gonna call a nicca, and you don't even have my number?" I shrugged and waved, leaving him standing in front of the elevator doors. I really wasn't into mixing business with pleasure.

By seven, my phone was ringing. It was a number that I didn't recognize. "Hello," I said.

"Yo, Milla. It's me."

"Me who?"

The deep voice laughed. "Me. KG. Stop frontin', ma. Ay, yo, look out your window right quick." I got up from my bed and walked downstairs toward the front door. I opened it and a damn stretch Rolls-Royce Ghost was parked in my driveway. The driver was standing outside the car.

"Really? KG? How did you get my address and number?" I knew that damn Cedrick probably gave it to him.

"Don't worry 'bout all that. Just have your pretty ass ready by ten."

Chapter 8

SUNNY-SOLÉ

I hated having to visit my king in prison. Not just because he didn't belong here, but having to deal with the hating-ass bitches at the visiting desk. My hair was bone straight, hanging to the middle of my back, and it swayed from side to side, mimicking the movement of my hips. I looked extra good for my king, getting as sexy as possible without being banned from entering the prison. Every time I came here, they threw shade and hated on me heavy. But, hey, if I saw a bitch as fly as me, I might hate too. So I wasn't really mad. It was more annoying than anything else.

The off-white Anthony Vaccarello one-piece pants suit I wore didn't fit skin tight, but the chiffon material clung to my ass just how he liked it. Showing every curve. I rocked gold-studded Giuseppe open toed booties, and, of course, my jewels were shining. Flawless.

"Remove your jewelry, ma'am, so it doesn't sound the alarm," this busted correction's officer bitch instructed. I rolled my eyes. I swear the BOP kept a hatin'-ass ho on their payroll.

"It's not going to beep. Trust me. I been doing this for a minute," I replied. My attitude expressed my true thoughts.

"Ma'am, only *real* jewelry doesn't trigger the machine. That is clearly costume jewelry you're wearing. So, please, to save us some time, just put the jewelry in the bowl." She shoved the bowl in my face, and I ignored her. I removed my shoes and put them in the bin. I didn't take my eyes off them. I didn't trust these broke, miserable overseers for one second. Once my shoes were safely in my view, I walked through the metal detector.

Silence!

There was nothing fake about what I wore. Especially when it came to my jewels. The look on her face was priceless. I let out a sarcastic chuckle before entering visitation. And there he was, waiting for me.

My husband was not just my husband; our love went beyond what the average couple considered as marriage. We were royalty to one another, and that is how we addressed each other all the time. I'm the Queen, he's the King, and our son is the Prince. I may not have had a crown or a scepter, but what I did have was a long reach, and my king kept a pack of wolves who moved at his command. I would do anything for him. And today, he would find out just how loyal and deep my love went.

"What up, Queen!" he said right before kissing me softly. "I missed you, baby." There was no other place I wanted to be other than in his presence. He was the best thing that ever happened to me. He had no idea what I'd done with the governor. I wasn't supposed to make this trip until the following week, but he called me and told me it was imperative that I visit with him immediately because he had some fucked-up news to tell me. I already knew what he had to say, and I was pretty sure that what I was about to tell him would blow his mind. The diva in me forced me to cross my legs and act dainty. But the gangsta in me had me ready to bring a war to the doorsteps of these slave masters who insisted on ruining my family.

"Yo, Queen, you're not gonna believe this." He shook his head in disbelief as he gripped my hand.

"I already know."

"You do? How, baby?" I looked around the visiting room to make sure nobody was listening.

"You're being transferred to state prison."

"On some trumped up, bullshit charges. I'm 'bout to—" I interrupted him.

"Listen to me, King. I set this whole situation up. I knew it wouldn't be easy. But I never prayed for life to be easy. I prayed for us to be strong. And I went and put the muscle on the right people. I met with that crooked-ass governor, the one that copped them jawns from us."

"I told you, Queen, no moves without kicking it with me, first. I hate that you're out there without me. I know you're a beast, but you gotta be careful. What happened?"

"While the king is down, the queen takes over the kingdom. You already know how we get down. I wasn't about to sit and let them railroad you like this. Those bitch-ass Feds stole our money, paid off the judge, and covered it all up. I told the governor to have you charged with a state case, and then he's going to pardon you, and we're out of the country before the Feds show up to pick you up again."

"Got damn, Queen, that's a helluva plan. One can never underestimate my queen."

"As we speak, he is meeting with the judge and setting her up. Getting her to confess. Once he hands me the recordings, I gave him my word that we won't expose the fact that he buys counterfeit money to cover up what he stole."

"That shit is genius. Just make sure you operate using all the mechanics and principles that I taught you, baby."

"Always. I know. Play the game of life like it's a game of chess. Study the moves, strategize, and execute."

"That's my queen."

I left the prison feeling confident that everything would go just as I planned. I was making shit happen. I had a meeting scheduled with the governor. I couldn't wait to hear what happened when he met with the judge. I started my hour and a half drive to Albany. I was boppin' my head to POWER 105.1, FM when they started talking about corruption in the system and how these judges needed to be scrutinized more before being given so much power. The radio station's topic definitely had my attention. I thought it was a weird coincidence that they were talking about the same issue that directly affected me.

Then the words of my king flashed in my mind. *"Queen, there are no coincidences. Everything is connected and related."* That philosophy made sense, but I knew there was an exception to every rule, and this is one of those times, surely. There was no way that the topic this afternoon had anything to do with Sunshine-Solé.

Or did it?

What I heard next required my full attention. I needed to pull off to the side of the road because I couldn't focus. I had to make sure I was hearing this right.

"Okay, let's play the clip again, for those of you that don't know what happened this morning," the radio personality said.

"So, how many of these cases have you ever actually taken serious, Judge?"

"None. It's all about the money. I get paid to lock up trash, and I do it. The details don't matter. You understand, Governor, don't you? I've heard that you go about things unorthodox as well."

Oh my God, it was really her! She admitted to being a snake. The radio commentators interrupted.

"Unbelievable! And everyone is praising the governor for his bold move to release to the people of New York and the United States, his wired conversation with an anonymous federal judge, where she boldly admits to corruption. He's guaranteed himself reelection with this one, and she's guaranteed a trip straight to prison."

My phone rang, and I almost missed the call. It was him.

"I did my part. Now destroy that video."

"Done!" I said, and hung up the phone.

Chapter 9

ESHE

"Wake the fuck up, nigga!" Jeremy said to the Secret Service agent. He was bandaged up in the bed. Jerry tapped him with his gun on the forehead. The man opened his eyes.

"Chill, Jerry. I've got this," I said, calming him down. I looked at the agent and stood beside his bed.

"What are you going to do to me?" he asked. His words were strong, but there was a hint of fear embedded in his tone.

"No, *we're* the ones asking the questions. If you want to stay alive, you need to tell me why you were planting dope in my office." He closed his eyes. "You're still breathing, but I can change that, if you'd like," I said, not believing the words myself.

"I don't have anything to say," he muttered. "You have no idea what's going on. We're all gonna be dead, thanks to you."

"Fine. Jerry, make it a quick death, and Marcellus, figure out how we'll get rid of the body." It didn't matter if I meant it or not. Jerry would take that as a pass to do his thing.

"Yes, ma'am," Marcellus said. I walked toward the door, and Jerry pulled out his P-80 and attached the silencer. The agent tried to move, but he was handcuffed to the bed. He struggled against the restraints.

"Okay, wait! Wait!" the agent said in defeat, hollering for my attention. I stopped in my tracks and turned to face him.

"I don't want to hurt you. I am no killer. I'm a businesswoman. But you obviously wanted to see me rot in prison. You need to tell me what the fuck is going on."

"Okay. Look," he said, short of breath. He was still in pain from the gunshot wound. "I was just following orders, doing my job. I was told that you and your company are a problem."

"What the hell are you talking about?" I asked, frustrated.

"Some very important people don't like what you're doing. You did a deal for a guy named Amikbogo. You remember that?"

"Yeah, that was about six months ago. And . . . the issue is?"

"He's an African Wall Street trader. Small time. Until he met you. Well, he made about $200 million in an oil trading deal that you set up, and now he's in pretty damn good with some crude oil suppliers."

"Okay, what's the problem with that?" I thought I saw a smile appear on his face. It had, but it wasn't because anything was funny.

"You really don't know, do you?" he chuckled. "He referred about ten other blacks to you, and they all made a few hundred million after you set up trade deals for them. Wall Street is not too happy about this. Never in history have so many . . . *minorities* infiltrated the private oil trading world. You're not welcome there." Now everything made sense. My business was a threat to the white status quo of wealth in America. I didn't even know I was impacting the world on such a major level. I had no place to go but up, and they wanted to stop my growth and bury me. What was I to do? I needed time to think. I stared at the wall in deep thought.

I replayed the Secret Service agents showing up at my office. That unexpected visit rattled me. Not many things had the power to unnerve me. Because I was raised with the knowledge that I'm a goddess, I considered myself quite fearless. I attributed my success to that mind-set. I created my own blessings and curses. And as I stood in this hotel room, I pondered what actions I had taken that led to this curse known as the Secret Service invading my life.

When they were in my office earlier, they had the nerve to say that the president would be in the area in a few days, and they were randomly visiting offices and residences whose windows faced the venue where the president would be speaking. Thanks to the agent handcuffed to the bed, I now knew they were full of shit. They asked to see the window in my office so they could make sure that their security plans were in proper order. I acted as surprised as one would expect any person who randomly got a visit from the president of the United States' security detail. If they'd known I had one of their own chained up in a hotel, I probably wouldn't have made it out of the building. The visit lasted for about five minutes. They took pictures of the office and the window directly behind my desk. We were over thirty stories high, and I knew this was bullshit. But I played along.

Marcellus snapped me out of my trance. "Boss Lady, we gotta figure out what we're going to do with him. We can't just leave him here like this. We either kill him and risk going to prison, or we let him go and guarantee we're going to prison."

"I can help you!" he said, interfering with our conversation.

"I never really agreed with what they were trying to do to you. But I took an oath. I can help you. I promise I can keep you out of prison if you let me go. I'll testify if you let me live. I give you my word."

"Shut the fuck up!" Jeremy yelled. The agent got quiet quick. I pinched the bridge of my nose, trying to figure out what to do. I couldn't keep this man here forever. And I couldn't leave him unattended because we risked getting caught up.

"Jerry, I need you to stay here with him for a few hours until I figure out what we're going to do next because—" A knock at the door interrupted my words.

"Room service!" a female voice said.

"No, thank you!"

"But we have to clean, ma'am." I looked through the peephole and saw a small Hispanic woman. I opened the door slightly, leaving the chain on.

"We'll be checking out soon. Please take this and—" I flew back against the wall. It felt like it was happening in slow motion. Someone kicked the door open, and it hit me so hard I nearly lost consciousness.

They came in, guns blazing. Masked men. A loud pain-filled sound colored the room. Jerry was busting back for a second, but his sudden silence scared me.

"Jerry!" I screamed. I couldn't see what was going on. Marcellus jumped on top of me, and I couldn't see if my brother was hurt.

As fast as it started, it stopped. "Let's go! Let's go! Now, now, now!" one of the masked men yelled. Then they ran out of the room. Marcellus got up, and I ran to Jerry's side. He was hit in the arm, just a flesh wound. But the agent . . . He was riddled with bullets and lay there dead.

They killed him.

Chapter 10

MILLA

Flash! Flash!

Paparazzi is out heavy.

"Baby, you good?" KG asked. I nodded and smiled, looking up at him. Even going out to dinner was a big deal. At first, I played hard to get, but after spending some time with him, he grew on me. And it was definitely in a major way. It didn't hurt that his mind was on point, and his money was getting longer by the day. He was worthy of Milla time, and I couldn't front; I liked him. He was definitely my type of guy, and these last few months had been great. There was only one issue . . . I wasn't used to this type of attention.

Cameras literally followed us everywhere. Always stalking us. It was like: *Damn, get a life!* King-G was cool about it, reminding me that they were just doing their job. What really tripped me out was that I was on the cover of several gossip and entertainment magazines as KG's "mystery woman." Maybe a mystery woman to certain folks, but the hood's most fabulous and elite circles knew all about me. I'd gotten many of them their first luxury cars and houses. So far, everything printed about me was either neutral or positive. But I knew how easily that could change.

After dinner, KG and I headed back to his place. I liked his home more than mine. He lived in Jamaica Estates, but what I really didn't understand was how he maintained the lifestyle he had prior to blowing up in the hip-hop world. He'd been living here for years. He said he always invested in real estate and other things since he was about eighteen. Said his mother and father taught him. I thought that was dope.

I took my shoes off and plopped down on the couch.

"Why are you getting comfortable?" he asked.

"What you mean?" I said, sitting up, on alert.

"I'm hungry. Your man wants to eat."

"Hungry? We just left the restaurant. You just ate."

"Who said I was hungry for food?" He smiled, and then I realized what his nasty ass was saying. I tossed a pillow at him.

"Mmmm," he moaned. I burst out laughing, and then got comfortable again on the couch. He took his shirt off, revealing nothing but perfectly cut muscles and a physique like he just did ten years up north. The only parts of his skin that weren't caramel were the parts that were covered in tattoos. I purposely did not look at him long, and he purposely stood directly in front of me. "I'll be upstairs," he said. That nigga knew exactly what he was doing to me. I wasn't going up there. Hell, no. I still hadn't had sex with him, and fortunately, he wasn't pushing the issue. But it was getting harder and harder not to give in. I refused to have sex with any man, unless I knew he was going to be my husband. I made some bad choices in the past, and wisdom had definitely found its way into my brain.

The following morning I didn't want to get out of bed, but I had to get to the office. I walked into work refreshed and wide-eyed. King-G had given me a complete body rub last night. That man! I felt good. Too good. He seemed almost too good to be true. As soon as I sat down at my desk, my boss called me to meet him in his office. *What the hell does he want?* He was smiling from ear to ear when I sat down in front of him.

"Milla, Milla, Milla. What can I say? You have not only impressed me, but also all the higher-ups. The level of business you are bringing in has really done this bank well. I just wanted to commend you."

"Thank you!" I simply said. There was more to this meeting, and I felt it. So when this young blond chick walked in to join us, I knew something was up.

"This is Britt Arat. She's been assigned as your assistant."

"Hello, Britt. How are you?" I said, smiling. We gripped hands and shook softly.

"Hi!" she said. No other words. *Okay! I can see that I'm not going to like this bitch.* Her jittery handshake and her reluctance to look me in the eyes had me on high alert. My daddy taught me that.

"I just have one question, Mr. Darding," I said, taking my seat again. "I already have an assistant. Not that I have anything against Britt, but is there an issue with Gina?"

"No, not at all. This move came from above me. They said it was mandatory."

"I see." I wrapped that meeting up as fast as I could. There was really nothing else to talk about. One of the many talents I was blessed with was a good third eye. I could see bullshit a mile away, and something wasn't right with this Britt Arat chick. I'm just sayin', two black chicks, Gina and I, were doing the biggest numbers in our division, and I felt like Britt was their way of breaking us up.

The next day, Britt started working with me. I walked over to her desk and asked her to meet me in my office. I had to train her on the way I liked things.

"Hi, Brit," I said, trying this again. "Are you ready to get started?"

"Pretty much," she said in a superdry tone. So dry, I wanted to ask her if the can of Diet Coke on her desk was full of sand.

"Okay, sweetheart, let me be very straight with you. You don't seem happy to be here. And that's okay. Because we can walk over to Mr. Darding's office and tell him you'd like to be transferred. Because I don't want anybody in my presence who really doesn't want to be there." My tone was direct and condescending.

"I'm sorry. I'm really sorry. It's just that, well . . . I liked my old job, and they moved me, saying that if I wanted to stay with this bank, then I didn't have a choice. So I was a little bit frustrated. I do apologize."

"Well, at least now I understand. It's all good. Loosen up a li'l bit. I'm cool and laid-back. You'll love working for me. But first things first . . . Every morning I have to have a fresh cup of black coffee on my desk. Two sugars."

"Got it!" she said, running off to fetch that coffee. When she came back, she set it on my desk and just stood there. I looked up at her.

"Thank you."

"You're welcome." She was still standing there looking curious.

"What?" I said, smiling. "Go ahead, ask me."

"I'm sorry." She giggled. "It's just . . . do you really date King-G?" *Here we go.* I chuckled.

"In a way. We're close friends."

"Just friends?" she asked.

"Yeah, just friends? That's it?" I heard a masculine voice ask.

The two of us looked up and there was King-G, standing in my office with a bouquet of roses.

"What are you doing here?" I asked, smiling. I looked outside my office and the entire company was at a standstill, staring at us.

"Can you, ummm, excuse us for a minute, Britt?"

"Sure, sure," she said, nodding. And then she left, almost tripping over her own feet.

He walked behind my desk and stood next to me. Then he bent down and kissed my cheek. My entire body reacted. He pulled something out of his pocket and set it down on my desk. Then he sat in the chair in front of me. I opened it. It was a check for $1 million. I looked at it, then at him.

"I need your help," he said.

"What do you want me to do with this?" I asked.

"I want to invest. Mutual funds, IRAs, stocks, bonds, futures, real estate, you name it. Handle it for me."

"King, this is a lot of money. I don't think—"

"Listen to me. This music shit is dope. I love what I do, but it may not last. The next big thing could come along tomorrow. My main concern is securing our future."

Did he just say "our" future? This was a bit much. I looked at the check, and then up at him.

"You're really serious, I see."

"As a crackhead on a mission."

"Very funny. But seriously, this is a lot of money to risk."

"I know. But I also know without risk, there is no reward. I'll see you when get off." And then he left.

Chapter 11

SUNNY-SOLÉ

Judge Brenda Doom disappeared. I heard through the grapevine that she'd been arrested, but quickly released and placed on house arrest. But where was the exoneration for my husband? Judge Doom's case was sealed, and her identity was hidden. Nobody knew that it was her. But I did. And I planned on letting the world know about it.

First and foremost, I was a woman of my word. I had to meet with Governor Wyzask and give him the final copy of the recording. He'd held up his end of the bargain and assisted me with getting Judge Brenda Doom to admit her wrongs. And my husband had finally been transferred. His pardon was pending. That meant a lot to me because I was doing all of this for my king.

We were meeting in a neutral place. At Niagara Falls in Canada. In case he tried something funny, I didn't want to be in a place where the United States had any jurisdiction. Right before I reached the border, my phone rang.

"Yeah," I said as I answered crudely.

"Look, I'm right at the border, but I just got a call from my office that if I cross in Canada while on official governing duty, I'll have to bring my security detail and explain why I'm spending taxpayers' money for a nonofficial trip. There's just too much red tape. We can meet right at the border." That muthafucka didn't care about taxpayers' money when he was stealing it. Whatever!

"All right, fine. Let's just get this over with. Where do you want to meet?"

"There's a park. It's Niagara Falls Community Park, actually, and it will come up in your navigation. How far away from the border are you?" he asked.

"Just about forty minutes."

"Do you wanna grab a bite to eat?"

"I'll see you there." I ended the call. I wasn't his friend, and I didn't want to have small talk with him. I was on a mission. And I wanted to get this done and over with. I wasn't going to chitchat with him over the phone. I floored my Maserati GranTurismo so I could get there just a bit sooner than expected. I was only about five minutes away, but I wanted to scope out the area before I got out of my car. You could never trust a man like Wyzask.

I couldn't miss the long, black, wool trench coat, leather gloves, and Stacy Adams shoes. The energy of a nervous man could be detected from a mile away. Even the birds and squirrels in the park seemed to sniff at him. Then they'd run off from the nasty odor of a foul soul. He stood when he saw me. All smiles. Phony ass. Who smiled when their life was interrupted the way I interrupted his? I didn't bother to smile back. This was business . . . the business of justice.

"Here you go," I said, passing him the flash drive.

"How do I know this is the only copy?"

"You don't. You do have my word, though. And I swear on my life, this is it. I want this to be over. Now, how long will it take for the commutation of my husband's state sentence to go through?" That smile on his face instantly vanished.

"It's bad enough you blackmailed me. What I did was wrong, but you were still wrong for selling counterfeit money. You didn't even sell it to me directly. I could've not done what you asked."

"I don't have anything else to say. Our business is done. Just make sure when that pardon comes across your desk, you sign it swiftly."

"I'm telling you, Mrs. Solé, if you try to cross me, I'll tell the authorities about your very illegal businesses and the way you blackmailed me."

"And it will be my word against yours. You can't prove it."

"And what makes you think that anybody would believe you?" he said, waving the flash-drive. Then he took two steps backward, away from me. By the time I realized what was happening I could only hope that it wasn't too late. I should have known that he was up to no good when he backed out of meeting up in Canada. Damn it! The Feds had us surrounded. I couldn't see them, but I knew they were there. I hoped they didn't realize that I had caught on to what was going down. I wasn't the type of chick to just lie down and die. I was only a few feet away from my car. If I could get in the car and drive just a few miles up, I could cross into Canada, and they would have no jurisdiction over me.

"They might not. But I think we're both better than this. You need to be able to go and live your life, and I'll live mine. We can put this behind us, don't you think?" Before he could answer me, I spotted a woman walking her dog.

"Excuse me, ma'am, but what a coincidence. I have the same dog. He's a Teacup Yorkie. He's in the car. Let me go grab him," I said. Then I looked at the governor. "Let me allow my dog to take a quick piss, and then we can go our separate ways." I jogged to my car, and that's when I saw them. They all came out of nowhere. A woman who pretended to be jogging, suddenly spoke into her wrist and began chasing me. A man who pretended to be watching his kids on the swing suddenly started running in my direction as well. There was another one, but I really didn't get a chance to see where the hell he'd come from.

I hit the automatic start on my car and jumped in. Flooring it, I took off for the crossing that would take me straight into Canada. I had to make this entire journey worth it. I was gonna get my husband out of prison or die trying. I was his ride or die. His one and only queen. I didn't come this far to get caught up.

The Canadian border was just up ahead of me. I looked in the rearview mirror and saw a sea of red lights.

They were behind me, but not right up on me. There had to be at least twenty police cars and FBI vehicles chasing me. I wasn't supposed to be the one running. I made a quick maneuver to switch lanes and I swear it felt like my car was on two wheels. There was no turning back now. It was do or die at this point. I pulled up to the border inspector.

"Identification please. Your passport." I handed it to him and looked in the rearview mirror once more. They were gaining. The man was almost done processing me, and then I heard his radio come alive. He looked at me and spoke back into the radio.

"Is there a problem?" I asked.

"Ma'am, you need to exit the vehicle."

"For what?"

"You need to exit the vehicle." I knew there couldn't be a warrant for my arrest just that fast. Technically, I didn't know who was really chasing me. So I had an excuse to run.

"Never mind!" I threw the car in reverse and backed up. I front ended the car behind me. "Get out of my way!" I screamed out of the window. The car moved just enough for me to get out of line. I jumped the divider in the middle of the eight-lane highway and started going in the direction toward home. I drove right past all the police who were just pulling up to the border station. I had to think fast. Then suddenly, out of nowhere, an entourage of police hit the highway. A helicopter seemed to manifest out of thin air. It was an FBI helicopter. Shit! My whip might have been able to do a lot of things, but outrunning a helicopter wasn't one of them.

I slowed the car and pulled over. I got out, raised my hands in the air, and dropped to my knees. It was over.

The queen was going down!

Chapter 12

ESHE

Before I could even wrap my mind around what was happening, I heard the sirens in the background.

"Come on. Let's get the fuck out of here, Boss Lady!" Marcellus said.

"No! The hallways are full of people."

"But nobody knows we're here. We can go."

"I'm not going on the run. You all can leave if you want. It's your choice. But I'm not because—"

The police arrived at our hotel suite door. Guns were drawn and cameras were rolling. There was a dead man riddled with bullet holes and handcuffed to the bed. Jerry was injured, and Marcellus was trying to tell the police that we were ambushed. It still didn't explain the dead man being handcuffed to the bed. This was a disaster. I raised my hands to show that I was unarmed and willing to surrender. Not to any crime, of course, but just showing good cause so I wouldn't get my head blown off.

We were all arrested and taken to the precinct. We hadn't been charged with anything . . . yet, but I wanted to make sure that we had the proper legal representation as we tackled what would be the biggest fight of our lives. I was taken into the interrogation room alone, and my brothers were taken individually as well.

"Ms. Aisha Haller, right? That's your name? But you go by Eshe?"

"That's correct."

"How old are you?"

"Why does that matter?"

"Are you going to answer the question?" he asked.

"I'm twenty-five."

"Just twenty-five, huh? That's pretty young to be worth what . . . almost ten million?"

"Something like that." The look of disgust on his face was enough to scare me, and I didn't scare easily. Something about a young black bitch with money frightened the hell out of people. Yeah, I was on my Cleopatra shit hard, and this white boy was definitely no Caesar.

"What were you doing at the hotel?"

"You just read to me my accolades, my accomplishments, right? So why do you think I would be stupid enough to sit here and talk to you without my attorney, when no matter what I say, you are looking for something to use against me."

"You think you're smart, Ms. Haller, but you're not. We're the smart guys. We are the ones who always have the last word."

"Whatever makes your dick hard, sir."

"Now, please explain to me why this man was cuffed to the bed and why he is dead."

"For the tenth time, I am telling you, I am not going to talk to you without my attorney. And I don't know why he's dead."

"You expect me to believe that?" the detective stated calmly.

"I really don't care what you believe. My story is not going to change, and we're not going to talk about anything else until my attorney gets here. So, please, stop wasting my time."

"Your boys, they already rolled over on you. They already told us what we need to know. So you might as well do the same and save yourself the same way they are saving their own asses." I started to laugh. They didn't know Jerry or Marcellus like I did. I'd put my life on it that they kept their mouths shut, and they knew it was the same on this end. We moved as a unit. There was no betrayal in this self-made family.

"Don't say another word, Eshe. Not another word." I smiled when my lawyer walked into the room. "I need a moment with my client." The detective walked out of the room.

"Eshe, what the fuck is going on here? I'm hearing about a body, an ambush with masked men, and a shootout. Your hotel suite had an IV unit and hospital equipment set up for a man who was handcuffed to a bed. I mean, this isn't looking good. Tell me what's going on so I can help you."

I exhaled. I didn't know where to start. "You're not going to believe this, but this is the 100 percent truth. This guy, the dead one, either worked with or for the Secret Service. He was planting drugs in my office, and I caught him red-handed. I had my gun on me, and I held him hostage until he told me what the hell he was doing. He said the Feds didn't like my business. Some crap about me making too many blacks rich." He looked at me as he tilted his head. "I know. I know it sounds crazy. But this is what he said. I had him in the room, and I handcuffed him to the bed railing. He agreed to testify on my behalf if I let him go. Before I could do it, some masked men kicked in the door and killed him. I swear that's what happened."

"Nothing else?"

"No!"

"But that doesn't make any sense. You expect me to believe that you manhandled a Secret Service agent, and you were able to handcuff him to a bed. All while holding him at gunpoint?"

"Yes. I made him handcuff himself."

"And you mean to tell me that Jeremy and Marcellus had nothing to do with this?"

"Nothing at all. They were just in the wrong place at the wrong time." There was a deep silence between us. But lawyer or not, I would never roll on my friends. I wasn't a rat, and I wasn't a snitch.

"Okay, well, that's the story we're going with." He shook his head and got up. He tapped on the window and two detectives came in. They sat down and waited for my attorney to speak.

"My client hasn't been charged with anything, so we're leaving."

"Not so fast. She's being charged with murder."

"On what grounds?"

"These guys can tell you better than I can." Two men walked in wearing black suits and flashing their badges. Of course, of course. The Secret Service.

"Well, well, well, I am not surprised to see you again, Agent . . ."

"Cox. Agent Cox."

"Okay, well, the first time I met you, Agent Cox, you were in my office. What day did you say the president is giving his speech? 'Cause I checked, and he's not scheduled to be around here any time soon. You lied to me, and you had no right to be in my office."

"And why do you suppose I would do a thing like that?" he asked.

"My client doesn't have another word to say to you. And you have no right to arrest her." Agent Cox dropped a stack of papers on the table in front of my attorney. My attorney looked at the first word: SEALED. "Why is this a sealed indictment?"

"You can find out from the judge at her arraignment. Let's go, Ms. Haller." One of them lifted my arm from the table, and I snatched it back.

"I can walk on my own."

"Suit yourself," he said as he pushed me back down into the chair. "Bring me the shackles." He put the shackles on my ankles and stood me up. "Now. With your smart mouth—walk!"

That was my last day of freedom.

Chapter 13

MILLA

Things were moving fast with King-G and me. He begged me to move into his place, and I reluctantly agreed. I was an independent type of chick, and I wasn't really feeling the idea of giving up my own personal space to move in with a nigga. But he was proving himself more and more each day. And his mannerisms, charm, and respect were showing me that he was something different.

He was very disciplined. Every day he woke up and ran a few miles. Then he went into his backyard and shadowboxed for half an hour with a trainer. Finally, he would come inside and shower and write music. He had a small studio in the crib. All of this was done before eight in the morning. He always had a gift for me too. I mean, every single day he came in the crib with something. If it wasn't a necklace, it was a watch. Another time it was a painting. I couldn't wait to see what it would be this morning.

I liked giving in to him in some ways, but one thing he asked me to do that I refused was quit my job. I was making more than half a mill a year just in commissions. That didn't include the side money I pulled in. There was no reason to quit. I enjoyed the lifestyle my career afforded me.

I got up and made him breakfast. He stood behind me and kissed my neck. He had to lean down a few inches because he was so big and tall. His physique was the hardest thing for me to resist. Sexually, the energy was crazy. He could have easily been a football player in the NFL, that's how ripped he was. But so far, I still held out, and he seemed to think it was funny. He continued to kiss on my neck. His hands wrapped around my waist from the back. I closed my eyes and leaned against him. He moved his hands farther down, slipped them into my panties and whispered in my ear.

"I see you all wet for daddy." He found a comfortable place to play and stayed there. This was the least I could do—let him see what awaited him if he continued to act right. "Got-damn, baby!" he said. "I see you got that wet-wet. You really trying to make me go crazy."

I didn't answer him. I was just enjoying the feeling. I felt myself about to climax right there in the kitchen. He was working magic. And then he pulled his fingers away.

"Nah, sweetheart. If I'm not getting none, you're not either." Then he backed away from me, laughing.

"Whatever!" I said. "Very funny."

"Baby, can you take off today?" he said as he sat down to eat his breakfast.

"I've got a bunch of closings. I can't."

"But I'm going on tour, and I don't want to be away from you for two long months and not get to spend the day with you."

"I know, but there is no way I can get out of work. I've gotta go. But I will try to get off early. I promise." He kissed me on my neck and rubbed his hands across my breasts.

"You know you want it," he whispered. I did. I couldn't front. But I made a vow to myself that I planned on keeping. It wasn't easy, though. Not when you had a fine-ass specimen like KG walking around half-naked every day.

I walked into my office ready to get busy. I had money on my mind. Not that I couldn't get whatever I wanted from King-G, but I liked getting my own. "Milla, you have a call on line 5; someone named Cedrick."

"Thanks, Brit." I answered the phone.

"Yo, Milla Winfrey. What-up!"

"Big Cedrick. How are you?"

"I just wanted you to know that I'm gonna be able to pay back half that loan on Friday. Your boy King-G is doing better numbers than I thought. I just wanted to thank you for helping me out. You put Platinum Records back on the map, baby. I owe you big time!"

"Nah, you don't owe me nothin'."

"As a matter of fact, I guess I don't. I just happened to introduce you to your future husband."

"Future husband?" I chuckled. "I wouldn't go that far. But he is a nice dude. So, yeah, you're good. That was a nice tip." We both laughed. I ended the call, feeling good. He proved to be responsible, and it really made me look good, getting an early payment like that. Plus, I only charged him 11 percent interest. The bank was lucky to get that. Those other numbers were crazy.

Brit Arat was back in my office with one of those gossip magazines.

"Hey, Milla, did you see the *InLife* magazine today?"

"No, I told you for the hundredth time, I don't read that crap."

"Well, you've gotta see this article."

"What article?"

"It's about King-G."

"There are a million articles about King. His album just went double platinum."

"Well, this is a little different. I think you need to read it." I waved her in, frustrated, of course, that she was interrupting me with this crap.

"What's so different about this one?" I asked.

"What is King's real name?" she asked in almost an accusatory tone.

"Kino Grafton. And why are you asking me that way?"

"Just curious." She wore a suspicious look that I didn't like. "I don't know. This here says something different about his name," she said, shaking her head.

"You're his girlfriend; don't act like you don't know." She dropped the article on my desk.

It read:

WHO IS THE REAL KING-G?

An unknown fact about America's favorite rapper is that his real name is Kino Gomez. His father, don Santiago Gomez, a Mexican immigrant, was the leader of the Gomez cartel. He moved his family to New York in 1985, during the heart of the crack explosion. He was a major supplier of cocaine and heroin. Santiago Gomez disappeared in 1995 when the Feds were looking for him. King-G's mother, an African American woman, also disappeared shortly after her husband. A concerned neighbor, Michelle Grafton, took Kino and his sister Nikita in, then eventually adopted them. It is believed that King-G is still tied to the Gomez cartel and . . .

I put the article down. This was some bullshit. Even if this was true, that didn't mean he was connected to the cartel. He was just a kid. Brit stood there watching my expression closely as I read the article. So I purposely didn't react. She folded her arms as though she was waiting for something.

"Boss wants to see you, by the way."

"For what?"

I got my answer soon enough. When I walked into his office, two other men were sitting there. They must have been from corporate.

"What's up, Mr. Darding? What can I do for you?"

"Milla, have a seat." His face was scrunched, and his arms were folded across his chest.

"Is something wrong, sir?" I asked as humbly as I could. I hated not being in the know.

"These are Agents Black and Yikes from the FBI. You're being indicted on charges of money laundering."

"Money laundering? What are you talking about?" I asked. Agent Black interrupted.

"You've been investing and washing money for your boyfriend, who has just been arrested for trafficking heroin and cocaine. Please stand and place your arms behind your back!"

You've gotta be fucking kidding me!

Chapter 14
SUNNY-SOLÉ

There was something about being locked up that heightened your senses. I could hear the birds chirping, and I could smell the rain. I was on the yard all by myself, exactly how I liked it. It was foggy and gloomy. Nobody came outside when the weather was like this. Well . . . nobody but this bitch Chalk, of course. She didn't speak, just stared most times. She damn near followed me all day. When I picked up my food tray, she lined up behind me. When I had to use the bathroom, so did she. When I went to laundry, Chalk's pale ass was right there. It drove me crazy.

It started raining, but that was fine with me because Chalk took off running back inside. *Good riddance! I don't feel like being bothered with none of these chicks today. This whole environment is for the birds. County jail sucks. The food is unidentifiable, and it comes in these five-compartment trays that sit on top of other five-compartment trays. The whole setup is on some low-grade, dirty shit. I absolutely hate it.*

After being outside for forty minutes, it was time for me to shower. I slipped on my shower shoes and stepped inside. I was happy to see I was the only one because the shower is communal with no dividers and six showerheads. I turned on the water and tried to go as fast as I could, as I did every day. I wanted to be in and out before anybody . . . damn! I talked too fast. Chalk, this too skinny little white girl from Albany, decided to shower as well. *What the hell is wrong with this bitch?* I turned my water off and started to dry.

"What does that tattoo mean?" she said.

"First of all, why are you even looking at me, Chalk? I don't need no bitch that I don't know looking at the tattoos above my ass."

"Sorry, I just—"

"You just *what?* Girl, focus on washing your own damn ass, please."

"Fine. Whatever!" I had no privacy in this damn place. The toilets didn't have dividers either. I saw more than a lifetime's worth of dirty pads being changed. And nothing was worse than two bitches taking a shit and having the time of their lives chilling on the toilet. Jail life was just different than anything else I ever imagined.

I stepped out of the shower and immediately sneezed. It's always cold because the air-conditioning runs on full blast all day long. They say it's to keep down the germs, but I know it's really because they just want to torture us. There is no reason I should see my own breath whenever I exhale. Especially indoors. What type of Antarctica shit is that?

I'm waiting to be sentenced. My last two dates were cancelled. I was pissed because this county shit was about to make me lose my mind. I knew I'd eventually be moved to a federal prison, but this was the slowest six months of my life. For this to be New York, it certainly was a hick town. This town was no place that any black person should ever feel comfortable walking around at night or being alone. No wonder some people only considered the "real" New York to be the five boroughs and Long Island. They couldn't pay me to live around here. The deer definitely outnumbered the people.

There were about fifty girls in the jail and only three of us were black. I wanted to hurry up and get sentenced to get this shit over with. My husband ended up getting transferred back to the Feds. Everything just went all wrong. My charge was bribery of a public official. I could get up to five years. All I could do was hope for the best. I didn't want to lose my house or my cars, and it was bad enough that all of this started because those FBI agents stole so much of my money. Every day I exercised and did my best to keep a strong mind. I wouldn't let them take my sanity as well. But being here, that was a daily struggle.

Seeing crackheads was one thing; that was a daily thing growing up. But these meth heads made the crackheads in my hood look like supermodels. They had no teeth, deteriorating skin, and slumping figures. Those chemicals were no joke, and it appeared to have been burning them alive from the inside out. It seemed like all the meth addicts in Upper New York had been gathered up and dumped right here in the pod with me. It was sad to see people on this level. They were in a zombielike state. This wasn't the place for them; they needed help.

"What's that smell?" I asked Linda, my bunkie.

"I don't know. But it stinks."

"Every morning around the same time, I smell that shit. It's horrible," I said, frowning up and shaking my head.

"That's Jenn. She's got chicken grease, baby powder, her meds, commissary painkillers, lemon juice, and some alcohol pads all in a bowl in the microwave."

"What?"

"She's heating it, then she's gonna roll it in the lettuce we got for lunch and smoke it."

"Knock it off, Hot Sauce. Stop lying."

"I swear. She does it all the time." I knew I was in the Twilight Zone for real now. I took a nap, trying to sleep the time away. I bought three blankets from some of the other ladies. I wasn't with this cold shit. It felt like as soon as I had dozed off, someone was tapping my bed. What now? A flashlight was beaming in my face. I squinted and blocked the light with my hand.

"Solé! Pack out!"

"Pack out? What do you mean?" I asked, confused.

"To get sentenced."

"At two in the morning?"

"The Feds are here now. So you're going with them. You got twenty minutes to get all your possessions together." I didn't plan on taking none of this shit with me. I gave it all away to the other ladies. I gathered up my things and walked out of the pod with the CO. Chalk stood there crying her eyes out. *Yeah, this bitch is definitely loony.*

My nerves were all over the place. I was handcuffed and shackled and placed in the back of an all-white unmarked van. We stopped at six other counties, picking up eight women in total. By the time they finished picking people up, it was close to five in the morning. Then we headed to Brooklyn, where I'd be going to court. I was taken into the bull pen. I'd been in here many times before. The shackles were taken off. I stood before the worst judge in the district, Judge Marvin Kramps, appointed by George W. Bush. My lawyer patted me on the shoulder and told me to relax; everything was going to be good. The plea I signed was for five years, but judges weren't bound by that. So all I could do was pray.

After going back and forth for about thirty minutes, finally, I was told to stand and was asked if I had anything to say. I only spoke about my son. I asked the judge to please take him into consideration. He was only one.

"Mrs. Solé, your case is one of a kind. I thought long and hard about an appropriate sentence, and I find that two years is sufficient for your crimes," Judge Kramps said.

I had to focus all my attention on my mouth, to keep it from curling up into a smile.

Chapter 15

ESHE

We were hit with two separate indictments. The first one was for murder. But after searching our office and going through our files, we got hit with a few money crimes: bank and wire fraud. We were up shit creek without a paddle.

After months of fighting, we were up for sentencing on the white-collar case. A Chase Bank official had just got sentenced to probation, and the amount involved in her case was $250 million. A quarter of a billion dollars. And the sentence was probation. Wow! So with my little $20 million case, I was sure I'd get the same or better. At least, that's what I told myself. The only difference between her and me is that she's ten years my senior, white, and it's about oh . . . 200 million more involved. I should get a slap on the wrist for making a few clients appear to be worth more than what's in their bank accounts. Nobody lost a penny. Nobody got robbed or duped. Just a little white lie on paper where the end justifies the means. No big deal, right?

It was my turn next to go before the judge for sentencing.

With my head held high, I walked into the courtroom and nodded at my family. Everybody was showing so much love. The presence of my great-grandmother really moved me. She smiled that beautiful ninety-five-year-old smile at me. I stood in front of the judge and listened to them talk about me as if I wasn't even there. My attorney tapped me on my shoulder and snapped me out of my trance.

"He wants you to say something," he whispered. I nodded.

"All I ask is that you have mercy on my staff. Marcellus and Jerry never did anything that I didn't ask them to. So if you have to give somebody time, give it to me," I said to the judge. I looked him dead in the eyes and spoke from my heart. I meant it too. I didn't want to see them go down. They were offered no jail time at all, if they would just cooperate against me. But they refused. Just like I knew they would. We were all facing twenty years. The crazy thing is, the murder charge didn't carry as much time as the fraud charge. They were two separate cases, and here we were being sentenced on the fraud case first. I was told I'd be called back out on a writ from prison to deal with the dead Secret Service agent situation. This was all some bullshit.

"That is noble of you to take responsibility. But it doesn't change the fact that they acted in collusion with you, Ms. Haller. Regardless, today is the day we deal with you and—" The judge was interrupted.

"Your Honor, I just want to remind you that Ms. Haller here was the boss. Had this been a drug case, she'd be getting the kingpin charge. So with that being said—"

"Don't interrupt me again!" the judge warned. "I know the details of this case. I know the facts."

"Of course, Your Honor, of course. My apologies." The presence of a black queen always unnerved muh'fuckas. He was worried because my statuelike presence and the confidence in my voice struck a nerve with the judge. I didn't scare easy. Prison was just something I would have to get used to.

"Okay, Ms. Haller, I've decided that an appropriate sentence will be 126 months. Ten and a half years in prison. I don't feel that you are remorseful for your wrongdoings. And the aggravating factors associated with this case don't sit too well with me. Best of luck!" I wanted to give him the finger. *Best of luck? What type of shit is that when you just sentenced me to a decade in prison for some bullshit?* I badly wanted to speak on how that agent got caught planting dope in my office. But if I did, it would give motive for his murder. It would create more problems than it would solve. So I decided not to say anything and take it like a G.

I walked into Danbury Federal Prison ready to be processed. I still had my $3,000 weave in my head, and I didn't plan on taking it out right now. They stripped me out and were sending me up to the unit. I almost made it out of R&D . . . until this black CO chick called me. "Excuse me, ma'am. Ma'am!" I didn't answer to that shit, so I just kept on walking. She jogged over to me and stood in front of me. "Who processed you?"

"One of your friends. I don't know y'all names."

"Well, whoever did it didn't realize you have in a weave." *Damn! Always has to be one.* "I need you to take that out."

"Can't I do it in the unit?"

"Technically, you can't even go in there with your hair weaved. It needs to come out now."

"What if I refuse?" Then she reached in her back pocket and pulled out a pair of sharp scissors.

"Then I'll use these and cut it out." She smiled. A devious, devilish smile that showcased her rotten-ass teeth.

"Give me something to help get it out," I said. I didn't want this chick touching me. The door clicked, and three more chicks entered the holding cell. I looked up at them.

"What-up?" one of them said.

"Hey," I said as I searched my head for the start of a track.

"You need some help?" one of them asked.

"I'm good," I said sharply. I wasn't in the mood for making friends.

"Come on, let me help you," one chick said.

"Yeah, I'll help you too," the other one added. "My name's Shelly." A pretty black girl with jet-black skin offered.

"And I'm Milla." An almond-toned, bright-eyed woman who looked well put together introduced herself.

Milla and Shelly sat behind me and started cutting my weave out. It took them about half an hour. The CO stood in front of the cell watching. I hated being watched.

"Thank you!" I said as I imagined what a hot mess I looked like. My hair was cornrowed. "CO, let me get a comb, please."

"My name is Officer Hayts. That is how you need to address me. And . . . you'll get to buy a comb on commissary. Let's go. And give me that hair so I can throw it away." Three thousand dollars' worth of hair in the trash. What a tragedy. I was steaming that the bitch wouldn't even give me a comb. I was worth millions of dollars just a few months ago, and now I was walking into the prison looking like a wild-headed jungle woman. Milla put her hand on my shoulder and shook her head.

"You're still a beautiful chick. Fuck all that hair. You don't need it," she said confidently.

"Thank you. I guess I needed to hear that."

"It's all good. But I understand. Trust me. I just happened to take mine out a few days before I got knocked."

"How long you have?" I asked.

"I hate to even say the words."

"Can't be worse than me. I got a decade."

"I got a decade plus two and half," she said sadly.

"Damn!"

"Drugs?"

"White collar. Money laundering—that I didn't even do."

"Damn, mine is white collar too. They burned us."

"That's an understatement."

"All right, ladies, enough with the chitchat. Pick up your bedrolls and let's go. You gotta get to your unit." She gave us our bed assignments. Our numbers were one digit off from each other, so hopefully, that meant we'd be sleeping close. Milla seemed to have a lot in common with me. Except her hair was laid, and mine looked like a bird's nest.

The next morning on Saturday, we were told to stand up for ten o'clock count. That same correction officer with the rotten teeth walked onto the unit to count us. When she walked past me, my mouth damn near hit the floor. I tapped the chick Milla, who happened to be my side bunkie, and pointed.

"Yo, is this bitch *serious* right now? This can't be legal. Who does that?" I said with my face screwed up. The right side of my mouth lifted, and I grilled her. Milla sat up to look, and she fell out laughing.

Yeah, this was *definitely* going to be a long-ass journey. The bitch, Officer Hayts, was rocking my weave!

Chapter 16

MILLA

"Can I borrow that comb, please, if you don't mind?" I asked one of the ladies in D-Dorm. That's where we'd be living for about three days until we got assigned to a cubicle. No doors, no real privacy. Some shit I had to get used to. She passed me a comb that was full of gray hair strands. *Gross.* I planned on going straight to the bathroom to wash this shit out.

"You can keep it," the woman said. "Nice to meet you. My name is Beedie." I shook her hand. She was an older white woman with salt-and-pepper gray hair, who had to be about sixty years old. She wasn't the only one. I saw another woman who had to be at least eighty. *What the hell could she have done?* I planned on asking her too. I turned my attention back to Beedie.

"Where do you want to work?" she asked.

"I have to work?" I asked with disappointment written all over my face.

"Everybody does. I'm one of the mentors here. I'll tell you all about this place and help you get set up." I handed Eshe the comb when she walked up so she could stop having a fit and fix her hair. Then I went and sat back down with Beedie.

"How long have you been here?" I asked her.

"Oh, just a couple of months, but staff likes me, so they gave me this decent job."

"If you don't mind me asking, Beedie, what are you here for?"

"Well . . ." she hesitated.

"I don't mean to pry. You just don't look like a criminal."

"Neither do you," she said, smiling. "I'm a retired lawyer. I'm really here because of one of my clients. But it's not a big deal. I only have about four months left. I got a year and a day."

"What's up with the day?" I asked, confused.

"When you get sentenced to just a straight year, you are not eligible for good-time. But anything over a year, you get good-time credit."

"Oh, I see."

"How much time did you get?"

"Twelve and a half years!"

"Oh my! That's awful, honey. I will pray for you because that breaks my heart. I hate to see so many young women getting so much time. It's ridiculous."

"Yes, it is." I tried not to talk about my time because it was so painful. But it made no sense for me to run from it, because it was my new reality.

"Town hall!" the officer yelled out. I left the D-Dorm and walked into the main area. It was the first time I got to see all the women I'd be living with up in here. Everybody was staring at me and whispering. I stared right back. *What the hell are they looking at? Aren't they all in here just like me?*

"What's going on?" I asked Beedie. Eshe stood next to us combing her hair.

"Town hall. The warden is going to speak," Beedie whispered.

A man walked in and stood next to the CO and folded his arms across his chest.

"Okay, listen up. My name is Warden Havick." The way the ladies stared at him you would have thought they were at a male strip club, and he was the main attraction. I walked up toward the front to get a better look, and *dayuuum!* He was fine as hell. Now I could see what they were all looking at. He stood about six foot three. His physique showcased a well fit body, and he rocked a perfectly tailored suit. He appeared to be about thirty-five. A young dude. He looked to be either mixed or Hispanic. But he was all of fine. Eshe walked up to me and whispered in my ear.

"Yeah, I see it too. He's all right. But he's still the police," she said as she rolled her eyes and placed her hands on her hips.

"You got a point."

"You ladies know what I expect from you. Honesty, integrity, and self-control. Treat the other ladies here with respect, and most of all, yourselves. We're looking for a few volunteers to clean R&D, visitation, and . . . my office. If you are interested." Before he could finish his sentence, about fifty hands went up. Thirsty bitches. I looked around in disbelief. He smiled devilishly. He was eating this bullshit up. "Put in a cop-out and you'll be considered. Also, I want to bring up what happened last night. Unacceptable. And once I find out who was responsible, you will answer directly to me. Have a good day, ladies." He then walked away. The unit was wide awake and in full effect.

I now officially knew two people, Eshe and Beedie. "What happened last night?" I asked Beedie.

"Somebody threw boiling hot honey on a girl's face."

"What?" My mouth flew open in shock.

"Yeah, her face damn near melted off!"

"Why?"

"Girlfriend drama. Come on, let me show you the TV room. You can hang out here until count time at four." Eshe joined us, and we walked into the TV room to chill. We were still being watched. The two new kids on the block. Three chicks followed us in there, and my eyes followed them. They sat right beside us.

"You new?" one of them asked me.

"Yeah."

"My friend seems to think you are Milla, King-G's girlfriend."

"Nah, you got me confused," I said, smiling. Then I turned back to face the television. I didn't feel like talking about it, and I didn't know these chicks from a can of paint. Then, of course, as if on a timer, the news came on featuring a story about Milla Davison, the girlfriend of King-G, reporting to prison to serve her twelve-and-a-half-year sentence. My face flashed across the screen. And now I was looking like a liar.

"I told you that was her, Mecca!" the other one said.

"Ay, yo, ma," Mecca said, tapping me again. She was a stocky, dark-skinned girl who wore straight back cornrows. I turned around and gave her my meanest ice grill face.

"You ain't gotta front to me or my girl. Ain't none of us trying to get your autograph. You just a regular bitch up in here." I was about to say something, but Eshe must have read my mind. She stood up.

"Hold up with all that bitch shit. She might not want nobody in her business."

"And who the fuck are you?"

"Don't matter. I'm just saying chill with all the disrespectful shit." A crowd had gathered at the doorway of the television room.

"Look, y'all," Mecca said. "It's King-G's bitch, and she got a bodyguard." Everybody laughed. Then suddenly, everybody backed away.

"Fuck going on in here?" a deep male voice yelled. He sounded more like a drill sergeant.

"That's Lieutenant Longwood. Stay away from him," Beedie warned.

"Why?" I asked. But she didn't answer. His big black ass was right up on us.

"Is there a problem?" he asked, breathing down my neck. His facial expression had, well, no expression at all. He couldn't be serious. His shoulders were abnormally broad. His skin was as black as the best Iranian oil, and his teeth were as white as drawing paper. His eyes, though, they sat too deep in his head. His nose spread wide like a rumor across his face. And he had the nerve to flare it when he spoke.

"No, no, Lieutenant. Everything is fine. Is there anything I can do for you?" Beedie asked, brownnosing.

"Yeah, you can keep it down in this bitch." I couldn't help myself. I laughed. This clown couldn't be serious. His neck snapped around so fast I thought it was going to detach from his body. "Something funny, little girl?" he said. I looked behind me to my left, and then to my right. "Hello?" he said, clapping his hands in my face. "I asked you a question."

"Oh. I didn't know you were talking to me. You said, *little girl*, and I was under the impression that everyone in federal prison was an adult." Beedie's eyes got beady for real. They looked like they were about to pop out of her head. And he looked like he was about to blow a fuse as well.

"I don't care who you are. But you are now property of the United States Bureau of Prisons. And if you ever disrespect me like that again, you *will* regret it." He stormed out, and the metal door closed behind him.

"Wheew! Yaaah!" Everybody clapped and cheered. I looked around, and they were all pumping fists and whistling. Beedie walked up to me.

"You stood up for yourself to Lieutenant Longwood. He's a real jerk, and everybody is scared of him. They're praising you. But now you're on his radar. Be careful!"

Great!

Chapter 17

SUNNY-SOLÉ

The bus pulled into the prison, and I couldn't wait to get the hell off this thing. It was hot, the air-conditioning had broken down about four hours ago, and the marshals driving the bus only played country music. Torture. Riding around handcuffed, chained, and shackled was like being placed in a barrel and dropped down a waterfall. You just moved around without much control.

I sat in a cage with one other chick, directly behind the driver's seat. The rest of the bus was packed with men. There were about eighty men and a total of six females. I had to pee. My bladder was about to explode. And the bumpy-ass road didn't make it any better.

"Excuse me!" I said. Neither one of the marshals turned around. "Hel—lo!" I said in a singsongy kind of tone. Finally, the one sitting in the first seat turned around. He screwed up his face and looked me up and down. I guess that was his way of asking me what I needed. "I have to use the bathroom."

"You have to wait," he said, immediately turning back the other way.

"It's been an entire day. How much longer? We've been through five different states. Through sixteen counties. I haven't washed my ass. I haven't brushed my teeth. All I'm asking is that I use the bathroom because I haven't in over six hours. I really have to pee."

"And I really need a raise. We all need things." The driver laughed, and the two of them bumped fists. I wanted to slip my cuffs off and stab them both. Every day I felt the animal side of me wanting to come out more and more. That's how angry he made me. I sucked up the urge to cry. I didn't want them to think I was weak. This was inhumane. I looked at the girl next to me. She couldn't be more than twenty-one.

"I have to go too!" she complained. "And I don't think I can hold it anymore," she whispered, frightened.

"Oh, hell, no! Y'all need to let us out of here," I said, yelling.

The driver looked at the other marshal and nodded. He got up and headed toward the back of the bus. There was a shower curtain type contraption back there. God only knew what was behind it.

"You first, Soléy. Let's go," he said as he unlocked the cage I was sitting in.

"Where am I going? I thought the bathroom in the back was broken."

"It is. But since you wanna keep whining, I got a solution." I walked toward the back, handcuffed and shackled. There was no door, only a curtain. I moved the curtain and there was a white bucket. "What the fuck?"

"Hurry up, you got one minute!" he said.

"Can you undo my cuffs?"

"Nope." How the hell was I supposed to use the bathroom over a bucket while chained up? I did my best. No way to wash my hands or anything else. This was hell. When I got back to my seat, the young lady was shaking her head.

"I'm sorry," she mouthed. I looked down. The seat was wet. She pissed. This ride couldn't get any worse. I didn't have a choice but to sit down next to her.

I could only imagine what a slave must have felt like being shackled like an animal. When the cuffs were removed I felt like I weighed less. They were heavy and seemed to have weighed down my soul.

After they processed me, I went back into the holding cell, waiting to be transferred up to my unit. An officer came over to me. "Before you leave, you need to take that weave out of your head." Her tag read, Officer Hayts.

"I don't have a weave in."

"Yeah, yeah, yeah. All you chicks come in here talking the same shit. Don't make me have to cut it out," she said, making two of her fingers mimic scissors.

Is this bitch crazy? "I'm telling you right now. Don't touch my head. This is all my hair." My hair cascaded down my back. It's always been long. What? Black chicks couldn't have long hair? What was the big deal? Haters! The story of my life. I ran my fingers through my hair and parted it down the middle with my finger. She watched and frowned up her face. I just laughed.

Upon entering the unit, I was told to report to D-Dorm. Another girl walked in with me. She's a beautiful girl with a warm and comforting face. I wasn't the only one to notice. I could see one of the male officers staring at her body and taking in her physique. She was just processed too and placed in D-Dorm as well.

"What's your name?"

"Jackie Gaines. You?"

"Sun-Solé."

"Hey, Sun-Solé, good to meet you." She shook my hand. "Have you ever been locked up before, Sun-Solé?"

"No. This is my first offense."

"Me too. I'm nervous."

"Don't be nervous. Look," I said, pointing. "You see that male officer over there checking you out?" Jackie and I both looked in his direction. To our surprise he didn't turn away or try to hide it. He just kept looking as if we were up in the club or something, and he was about to come over and holler.

"Wow, he's bold!" Jackie said. We both laughed.

"Is something funny, ladies?" he said, approaching us.

"Oh, I didn't know we weren't allowed to laugh," I said.

"Did I say you could talk?"

"Umm . . . didn't you just ask me if something was funny?" I reminded him. He was about to say something, but thought better of it. I had him, and he knew it. He turned his attention from me to Jackie.

"Come with me, Ms. Gaines."

"Where?"

"It's a direct order. Don't question me." She looked at me, and I shrugged. It was only her and me in D-Dorm at this time. He pulled her over to the side and talked in a hushed tone. But there was no conversation I could not hear if it was within earshot. He spoke different to her than he'd spoken just a few moments ago.

"Are you pregnant? That's what your file says," he said softly.

"Umm, yes. About six weeks." Jackie put her head down. He touched the small of her back.

"Well, if you need anything, just ask for me. My name is Lieutenant Longwood." He left.

"Girl, I didn't know you were pregnant. Congratulations."

"Thank you!" she said. Then she began to cry.

"Oh no, honey. You okay?"

"It's just that I never imagined having a baby in prison. In prison? This is just too much. The judge refused to let me surrender after I had the baby. It's just fucked up," she said, still crying. I hugged her. Our moment was interrupted as the ladies started coming back into the D-Dorm. One girl came over to me and introduced herself.

"Hey, what's up, y'all? My name is Eshe. I'm filling in for my friend Beedie. She basically gets new people settled in, but she had to go to the doctor. She'll be back soon." Eshe seemed cool. She was a tall, brown-skinned girl with a big warm smile. I shook her hand and so did Jackie.

"Where is 14 Upper? That's my bed assignment," Sun-Solé said. Eshe pointed. "And what about 6 Upper? That's Jackie's." Eshe pointed to another top bunk.

"But she's pregnant. I don't think she should be on a top bunk."

"Oh. Damn. They know better than to assign you to a top bunk. I'll take you to the officer to get it changed. In the meantime, they're about to serve lunch, so let me show you where we eat."

"I don't feel too good, Eshe. I think I'll lie down," Jackie said.

"Okay, cool. You can lie on my bed in the meantime. I'm on a bottom bunk." Eshe spread out a sheet and told Jackie to lie on it. That was nice of her. We left Jackie on the bunk and proceeded to the dining hall. We sat at a table with three other chicks. The food was all right. Chicken and rice. The chicken was in big chunks, lightly seasoned with white rice and veggies.

"Not too bad," I said as I ate.

"You can have some of my commissary until next week, if you need it. Just pay me back when you can," Eshe offered.

"I should be straight, but thanks," I said. Our conversation was interrupted when the door popped.

"That's probably Beedie coming back. I don't think there are any more new commits today." All the ladies watched the door, and the cafeteria got quiet. Then an older white woman rounded the corner.

"Yeah, it's just Beedie," Eshe said as she continued to eat, and everybody started eating and talking again.

Everybody but me. I rose to my feet and dropped my fork.

"What's wrong?" Eshe asked.

"Who is that again?" I pinched the bridge of my nose, trying to gain some composure.

"Beedie. Her name is Beedie."

"What's her real name?"

"Actually, funny you ask that. She never wears an ID card, and the guards call her Beedie as well. But she recently told me her name. It's Brenda Doom. Why?"

My heart fluttered. *Coudn't be!* I immediately jumped over the table and ran like a stallion in a race. I could hear the faint echo of Eshe's voice telling me to stop. But I was on a mission. This *bitch*. The real Judge Brenda Doom was right here. And all I could see was red. The Feds fucked up putting us in the same prison. She didn't know what hit her when my fist collided with her face. She fell backward and hit the floor. Blood immediately poured from her nose.

"Oh shit! Somebody fuckin' up the nice old white lady!" one of the girls shouted. I climbed on top of her and smashed my fist into her body repeatedly.

"Help! Help!" she screamed. "Somebody!" They knew that I was too mad for this to be about nothing, so everyone minded their own business. Nobody pulled me off of her, and I didn't plan on stopping either!

Chapter 18

ESHE

"Yo, chill!" I screamed. I did the best I could to pull this new chick Sun-Solé off Beedie. Damn, Beedie got dat ass waxed. The guards finally ran in and attempted to separate them. Sun-Solé was still screaming, and guards poured into the unit like a can of spilled beans. They were every damn place. "Everybody report to your bunks now!" one of the female officers said.

"You crooked-ass old bitch. Every time I see you I'ma beat dat ass. *Every time!* You hear me?" Sun-Solé hollered as they pulled her off Beedie. Just as they were almost completely separated, Sun-Solé kicked her leg up and caught Beedie in the head. She fell unconscious instantly.

"Oh shit!" one of the guards said. Some charges were definitely going to filed. Hopefully not homicide, because the lady looked dead. I hope she didn't kill the old lady. Lieutenant Longwood burst through the doors.

"Everybody shut the hell up!" he said, sounding like a drill sergeant. "Bring Williamson to me." She was cuffed and being held by two officers. They had to drag her away because she was in such a rage. The tips of her toes scraped the floor as they pulled her toward the lieutenant. She went into the office with him while medical came and got Beedie. Or should I say, the judge.

"That was crazy. I would have never thought Beedie was a judge," Milla said, standing next to my bed.

"I know, right? I guess you just never know who the hell is up in here."

"I wish I could get my hands on my judge," Nay-Nay added. She was a heavyset, light-skinned girl with freckles. She slept in the bunk beside me. Cool chick from what I could see.

"I think most people feel that way," I said.

"No, you ladies speak for yourselves," Nay-Nay's bunkie added. "You break the law, you pay the price. The judge is only doing their job," Keira Marx stated. She was a stuck-up Spanish girl who had long, curly hair that fell below her waist.

"Wait a minute, Kiera . . . aren't you here for something you *didn't* do?" Milla asked.

"I mean, well, yeah, but—"

"White folks always side with other whites, even when they've been wronged. We can learn a lot from that. Maybe if we stuck together like them, we wouldn't go through half the shit we go through," I said. One thing they would learn about me real quick was that I kept it real all the time, and I didn't sugarcoat shit. Kiera looked to be about thirty. They say she was a medical biller, and her boss was scamming Medicaid. The entire company went down after her boss blamed everything on the employees. There was no justice in her case; yet, she was defending the judge and the system. I just didn't get it. Nobody as much as inquired about Sun-Solé. She was new and didn't have any friends yet. But I couldn't get her off my mind. I knew she was probably upset about being in the hole, but at the same time, it must've felt nice to get some hits off on a judge. One who did you dirty, at that. I pulled out a piece of paper and decided to write her a note:

> *Keep your head up, girl. I think you're a strong chick. I went to*
>
> *your locker and got your stuff. Some of the ladies acted like*
>
> *they were going to take your things, so I hid it in my property.*
>
> *Hold your head up.*

Milla told me to send the note on second shift with the guard. They say he's cool, and he'll pass it on his way home. When he came in, I told him to please get it to her. He nodded and went about his business.

The next morning, I stood on the line for breakfast. To my surprise, the food was decent. Eggs and bagels with cream cheese.

"Jackson 054, Jackson 054, you have a visit!" the guard yelled. Jackson, a short, stocky girl with wild-looking hair jumped up from her bed and started running toward Milla's and my table.

"Yo, new girl."

"Her name is Eshe, and what do you want? Don't you need to get ready for your visit?"

"You know what I need. I need some chocolate. You got a Snickers?"

"Girl, why do you always ask for a Snickers right before your visit?"

"I got one. Somebody gave it to me yesterday. Come on," I said to Jackson. Maybe chocolate calmed her nerves before a visit. We walked over to my locker so I could give her the Snickers. When I turned to hand it to her, she had her pants and panties down.

"Girl, what the fuck?" I said. She snatched the Snickers from me and set it in a cup of hot water. She took it out after a few seconds and started smearing the melted chocolate in her panties. The peanuts made it look clumpy. It was disgusting, and I wanted to vomit.

She looked around, and then began to whisper, "As soon as they take us to the back to strip us out, I'll be quick to pull my panties down. The female guard will start gagging. The guards won't search me if they think I'm the shitty girl. Then I can bring in whatever I want." She continued to smear the chocolate in her drawers, and then pulled them back up. Disgusting. She smiled and ran toward the door to have her visit. These people were crazy as hell.

I walked back to the table where Milla was sitting and picked up my tray. "You're not going to eat?" she asked.

"No appetite. Not anymore. Not after what I just saw." I didn't even want to talk about the shit I just witnessed. An hour later, Jackson 054 returned from her visit. She went straight to the bathroom. She was back and not in the hole, so obviously, her little scandal worked. When she came out of the bathroom she washed her hands, and then walked straight to me.

"Good looking earlier," she said. "I got you these for your help." She tried to hand me a pair of cubic zirconia earrings.

"Thanks, but no thanks," I said, looking at those earrings. I didn't know where the hell she'd stashed them to get them back up in here, but I definitely was *not* interested in possibly putting something that was up her ass, or any place else, into my ears. No, thank you!

"You sure you don't want them?"

"I'm sure. But that was thoughtful. You're bolder than me. I'm just trying to do my time and go home."

"I feel you. But I gotta do what I gotta do. I don't have nobody outside to take care of me. I take care of myself. They only pay us five dollars and a quarter a month. Who can live off of that? Whether you're in prison or not, that's some bullshit. I hustle, having my people bring shit up here that the ladies need and I get paid for it. So if you ever need anything, Eshe, you let me know, and I got you. Just make sure it's nothing bigger than a soda can." Then she winked.

A soda can? I hoped to God this bitch wasn't sticking nothing up her ass or va-jay-jay the size of a soda can. I didn't even wanna know, honestly.

I wondered what my brothers were up to and how they were holding up in prison. I knew that men's prisons were much, much worse than female prisons. I thought about them a lot. I also knew that this wasn't over. We still had to be sentenced on this bogus murder charge. A murder we did not commit. Something had to give. I didn't have any more money. The Feds took it all in a forfeiture. I had too much pride to ask my family for anything. I was a multimillionaire, and I planned to keep that status, even if it was only in my mind. I had to find a way to survive in here, and I would make a way, one way or another.

Chapter 19
MILLA

Milla,

> *Baby, I am so sorry this happened. There is so much I need to tell you that I didn't have a chance to. I know you probably hate me right now. But I want you to know that I love you, and we are going to get through this. I'm going to put some bread on your books this week. It should hold you down for a minute. I hope you can forgive me, baby. I love you so much.*
>
> *I know you don't know yet, but I just got sentenced to life for a drug conspiracy. Don't worry, I'm a man. I can handle it. Just hold your head up and know that I truly love you.*

Love

King-G

I read the letter over and over again. I didn't know what to think about all of this. This couldn't be possible. A life sentence? For drugs? A conspiracy at that! My heart fluttered at the thought of KG telling me how much he loves me. But the reality of the situation is foul. I wish I could call the post office and take my mail back. I just went off on him complaining about getting a twelve-piece for him. But now that time seemed like nothing compared to what he got. I didn't understand how such a sentence was even legal. No murder. No bodily harm. No rape. Just a drug conspiracy. This just wasn't right.

A tear fell from my eye. Followed by another one. Then a whole team of them claimed territory on my face. My life will never be the same. I couldn't even provide for myself right now. Just a few months ago, I was making more money than the average person ever dreamed of, and now, every dime I ever made was being scrutinized and criticized like I was some brazen criminal. To make matters worse, I didn't even know his money was "supposedly" drug money. And even if it had been, my bank, my employer, was down with it. They were money hungry and used me to make a way for it to happen. Yet, I was the only one in trouble. The whole thing just didn't sit right with me.

I saw the chick Eshe walking in my direction, so I slid the letter under my pillow and wiped my eyes.

"You all right?" she asked.

"Yeah, I'm good. Just life, you know. Knowing that I am going to be doing all this time ain't easy."

"Tell me about it. I know the feeling. I got over ten years. And I'm still facing more time because I have a case still pending. The system ain't right. It's unfair."

"You're preaching to the choir, girl." The unit door popped, interrupting our conversation. Everybody looked up to see who was coming in. It was the chick Sun-Solé. How did she get out of the hole so fast? She spotted Eshe and me sitting on my bunk and walked straight to us, still wearing orange.

"How did you get out?" I asked.

"Technicalities. I threatened to sue them for putting me and the bitch on the same unit. We have a separatees, and the prison carelessly ignored it. So, technically, it wasn't my fault. They're at fault. They let me out of there real quick once they realized that I knew what I was talking about. My husband is locked up, so I know the game."

"That's good. But try not to fight anybody else," I added.

"Right!" Eshe agreed. She waved us off, as if there was no guarantee that wouldn't happen again if the right bitch came along.

"So let me tell you what happened while I was there. You know the girl Jackie Gaines, the one who's pregnant?"

"Yeah?" I said.

"Is she back? Have y'all seen her?"

"Back from where?"

"The ambulance came and got her last night. She fell out while she was cleaning the SHU."

"Damn, I hope she's okay. Her and the baby."

"I know, right? Well, Lieutenant Longwood rode in the ambulance with her."

"I think he likes her," Eshe said.

"Think? I *know* he does. You should see the way he looks at her," Sun-Solé said. "But anyway, the warden is the cool one. He's the one that personally let me out of the hole and apologized for the mishap. He said he doesn't know how his staff overlooked the separation requirement for me and Judge Doom. He said the fight wouldn't go on my record. Only because he's cute I let it go." The three of us laughed. Our girl talk was interrupted by the unit officer coming on the floor.

"Sun-Solé, get two other inmates and go down to visitation."

"But it's not visitation hours."

"No shit. The warden wants you to clean it up."

"Come with me, Queens."

"Nah, I don't do the cleanup thing," Eshe said, turning up her nose.

"Me either. Especially not after no strangers, like I'm somebody's maid."

"Y'all are trippin'! Do I look like Molly myself? This is just a way for us to get off the unit and get a few extra things. Let's be smart," Sun-Solé said. She had a point, I guess.

"All right. Fuck it. But only if it's only us three."

"Cool."

The three of us went down to the visitation room. It was empty and quiet. The officer locked us in and told us we had to be done in two hours. "So what are we supposed to be doing?" I asked, putting my hands on my hips.

"Shit, I don't know. Where do they keep the cleaning supplies?" Eshe inquired.

"Maybe in here," Sun-Solé suggested, pointing to a nondescript door at the other side of the visiting room. She cracked it open and quickly closed it. "Shit, that's the door leading to the mailroom. I can't believe they left this unlocked," she whispered.

"Can you see the front door from there, 'cause I'm tempted to walk right up outta here," I said. We covered our mouths, laughing.

"Oh shit! I hear somebody in there!" Sun-Solé said and she closed it partially.

"Who was it?"

"I don't know; sounds like Lieutenant Longwood. And he's talking in a hushed tone," Sun-Solé said.

"Girl, we need to mind our business. I'm not trying to have no problems with these people. Let's just sweep and mop these floors and get the hell out of here."

"I kind of want to know who's up in there too. Looks kind of shady to me," Eshe added. I rolled my eyes. These chicks were crazy.

"I'ma go up in there," Sun-Solé said.

"Bitch, is you crazy?" I asked. She had me talking all the way ghetto by now. "You not about to go up in there. Hell, no!"

"I can crawl," Sun-Solé said.

"Well, if you go, I'm coming too. I wanna see," Eshe added.

"I know y'all are joking right now."

"Look, me and Eshe will go. Milla, you be the lookout!"

"Oh my God! I'm not playing with—" Before I could finish my sentence, they were gone, crawling around the mailroom. *What the fuck!* My heart was racing. They had more balls than me. I looked at the clock. Three minutes passed, and they still weren't back yet. Then the unimaginable happened. The guard came back to check on us.

"Everything all right in here?" she said as she turned on the lights.

"Yes, everything is fine."

"Where are those other two?"

"Ummm, the warden came and got them a few minutes ago."

"What? I hate this job. How the hell are we supposed to keep up with y'all when they never tell us what's going on? Okay, whatever. I'm headed up to his office to see what work detail he has them doing. I'll be back to check on you again." She stepped out.

I ran over to the mailroom door and cracked it. "Get y'all asses back in here!" I yelled in a stern whisper. They came crawling back into the visiting room. By the stone look on their faces, I knew something had gone down.

"Listen, the guard came to check on us. I told her you all went with the warden. What the hell is going to happen when she sees the warden, and he doesn't remember taking you out?"

"Calm down, girl. Let me tell you what's happening up in there."

"What?"

"Prego, that girl Jackie Gaines—her and Lieutenant Longwood are in there fucking. They got music on and everything. We saw it!"

"Get the fuck outta here!"

"I swear. There is a little space in the corner, and there is an inmate mattress on the floor."

"You lying!" I said, handing each of them a mop.

"Nah, I saw it too," Eshe affirmed.

"So let me get this right. This muthafucka got one of the mattresses from the housing unit down on the floor in the mailroom fucking an inmate?"

Suddenly the door opened from the mailroom. His pants weren't even fixed. "What the hell y'all doing up in here?"

"What does it look like? Cleaning!" Sun-Solé said.

"There you go with that smart-ass mouth. Who authorized you all to be down here at this hour?"

"The warden!"

Just then, the officer was back.

"I thought you two went with the warden? Where were you?"

"We were waiting in the back of visitation, but nobody ever came back for us. We've been in here," Eshe said.

"Sorry, I misspoke earlier. I thought they went out, but they were waiting to be taken to the next area to clean. I guess he changed his mind. Or maybe it was the lieutenant," she said, looking at Longwood. He didn't say a word. He couldn't. "Look, I'm new. I'm sorry. I may have misspoken." The officer waved Eshe off in frustration before she continued.

"Well, hurry up in here so I can get you ladies back up to your unit before count time." Then the officer left again. I looked at Eshe, who cleaned up our situation with ease. She was definitely a jewel. Quick on her feet. The three of us now had information that could be used to our advantage, if necessary. I planned to sit on it and wait until it would be beneficial to us. This is what happens when you put a bunch of clever women in a cage together.

Chapter 20
SUNNY-SOLÉ

That time in the hole was needed. I had a moment to think about my situation. What were the odds of this bitch being at the same prison as me? Whatever the reason, I was grateful that I got to put hands on the old witch. She stole from me. Not just my money, but my life. She's the reason I am separated from my king and my prince. Unacceptable.

My method of trying to handle it may have been a little . . . well, unorthodox, but there was nothing I wouldn't do for my family. Family comes first and always will.

I was learning the ropes of this prison shit quick. Over the last few months, I bonded with Eshe and Milla heavy. We'd only known each other for a few months, but it felt like years. My bunkie, this chick named Munchie, was a real man in a woman's body. She was a straight stud. She was also the neatest person I'd ever met. I loved that about her. She was a cleaning machine, and I didn't have to lift a finger in our room. But what I didn't like was the fact that she woke up at five in the morning to start. It was not the quietest endeavor.

"Ay, yo, bunkie, can I put your shoes under the bed for now?"

"Munchie, it's just after five. I don't give a damn what you do. I'm asleep."

"Listen, today is a special day," she said, ignoring me.

"Why?"

"You know why! Don't even act like that."

"Oh shit. It's today?"

"You know it."

Today was my bunkie's wedding. And I'm not talking about a wedding through the BOP. I'm talking about a real prison wedding. Organized, catered, and conducted by inmates. Her chick lived down the hall. They've been together for the last four years from what I was told. Munchie's got thirty-five years, and her soon-to-be prison wife has twenty more to go. Veronica's her name. I thought this was cool and whatever worked for them, worked for me. Veronica came in the room and Munchie kissed her passionately.

Munchie pulled out what used to be a white sheet, and when she unfolded it, I could see it was now a wedding dress for Veronica.

"You gotta be kidding me! Y'all really 'bout to do this shit?" I said.

"Yup! Be on the yard at five today for the ceremony. Right after count time."

"Who's officiating? Who's the preacher?"

"We're still working on that." This shit was too funny. But I had an idea.

"I know who'll do it for you. She's working on her seminary degree right now. She'd be honored."

"Who?"

"Milla!"

"Milla? Girl, bye!" Veronica burst out laughing.

"Come on, let's go talk to Eshe. She can convince Milla of anything." We woke Eshe up, and I told her my idea about Milla officiating the wedding today on the yard. She fell out laughing.

"Bitch, you know good and well Milla ain't about to do that shit. She's into church, and her homophobic ass is not about to do no fake-ass ceremony at a jailhouse lesbian wedding."

"We'll see about that."

We walked down to Milla's room to wake her up. It was early as hell, but she needed to prepare her speech for today's ceremony. The thought of that was funny.

"What do you want, Sun-Solé?" she asked in a groggy tone.

"Why it gotta be Sun-Solé? You see Eshe standing here too!"

"Eshe would not be in here this early unless you dragged her," Milla said accusingly.

"Girl, just get up, we need to talk to you about something." Milla sat up on her bunk and screw faced both of us.

"What the hell y'all bitches want?"

"You got a job to do today. An important one."

"What are y'all talking about? It's the weekend. I'm chillin'. I'm not going on no cleanup, covert spy missions with neither one of y'all today," she said, pointing her finger at us. I knew she was talking about me, but I didn't care. I always had to know what was going on around here, and they were always going to be my witnesses.

"Veronica and my bunkie are getting married today, and they need you to be the minister at their wedding." The room got silent. Then Milla burst into laughter.

"What's so funny?" I asked.

"You! Y'all play too much, yo. For real, can I go back to sleep now?"

"We're dead serious. Who else would be better, Ms. Degree in Apolostethics."

"It's *apologetics*. Look it up, the defending of the Christian faith," Milla said assertively.

"Whatever. You know I ain't into that shit," Eshe said. "All I know is these bitches wanna get married, and they need somebody to run the ceremony. Who other than you?"

"Hell nah! Not me. You know I don't support that lifestyle. I mean . . . I don't have no quarrels with how muh'fuckas choose to live their lives, but I don't have to be no part of it."

"Oh, so that's how you feel?"

"Yuup!"

"Well, what if I told you I get me some tongue action every now and then? Would you have a problem with *that?*" Milla twisted up her face and looked at me with disgust, and then started praying. Eshe was cracking up.

"Lord, please touch my ratchet-ass friends, for they know not what they do. In the name of Jesus I ask—"

"Milla, please. Girl, be quiet. Just do the damn ceremony," Eshe said.

"No. Actually . . . Let me rephrase that. *Hell,* no!"

"So, you're saying your God don't know what he's doing? He makes mistakes? You know my bunkie has been a man in a woman's body all her life. How is that her fault? She was born that way. You people preach one thing and do another. If we're a reflection of God, then we are in every way, even the shit you don't like. For real, that's wack for you to act like that. You a homophobe, fam'. I didn't think you would be that way. Of all people, Milla!" Eshe said. "Come on, Sun-Solé. Let's go find a *real* woman of God to handle this." Eshe winked at me as we started to walk out of the room.

Milla jumped down off her bunk. "Really, so y'all resorting to reverse psychology now? I'll do the stupid ceremony, but if I'm going to hell, y'all bitches coming with me."

"You couldn't get rid of me if you wanted. I'll be right there with some Versace shades on."

Everybody was cooking for this wedding. The menu was off the chain. We had fried chicken wings. We stole some flour from the kitchen and used crushed crackers to supplement what we didn't have. They deep-fried it in the microwave in a plant pot. We had lo mein that could compete with any New York City Chinese restaurant. But ours was made from Ramen noodles and soy sauce and were sautéed in plastic bags laid out in a cardboard box. The mackerel patties melted in your mouth, and we had fried Thai noodles made from pressed rice and mayonnaise. And, of course, our famous potato logs—crushed chips, moistened and turned into a dough, then rolled out and stuffed with every meat known to man and enough cheese to clog every artery in the United States.

And then there was the wedding cake. We hired Paris. She wanted two books of stamps to be our baker for the evening. She used cream cheese and pudding for frosting, and cookies for batter. And to say the cake looked like a Carvel Special was still not doing it justice.

Everybody gathered on the yard. Even the people my bunkie didn't deal with. But it was a big event and something to keep us occupied. What really got me were the outfits. A couple of contraband scissors, needle, thread, yarn, and prison clothes could do a whole lot if you had the skill. We, the guests, had put some rice in socks and everybody was going to throw it at the end of the ceremony.

There was an entire wedding party with matching dresses and all. And the bride and groom weren't playing any games. They looked the full part. I couldn't believe that Milla actually showed up.

"Y'all know y'all owe me for this shit here," Milla warned.

"Man, this is crazy. You see all these people?" I said as I looked around at all the people on the yard. The lookout was on deck to let us know if the guards were coming. So far, so good. We had to move quick.

"All right, come on. Step up," Milla said to the wedding party.

"Don't forget to mention the rings. We got rings too!" the groom reminded Milla. I wanted to burst out laughing, but I held it in.

"Anyway, good evening, everybody. Today, we celebrate the love between Veronica and Munchie. At first, I wasn't going to do this ceremony. My beliefs don't align with everything going on here today. But then when I thought about it, I asked myself, what is God? And is God not love?" There were a whole bunch of "amens" and "I know that's rights" and "tell it, girl." I was proud of Milla. She continued. "So I say that to say, even in the hells of incarceration, we still find a way to enjoy the gift of love. The gift of life. I hope that you all continue to be happy and celebrate love because—"

"Hold up!" Shanice said, interrupting the ceremony. Shanice is the bunkie of the bride, Veronica. "I just came back from my visit. I've been gone all day, and this is what I come back to? Really?"

"What's the problem, Shanice?" I asked, sensing that shit was about to get all bad.

"The problem, Sun-Solé, if you must know, is fake-ass Veronica. Just last night she was all up in my bed, laid up with me, saying how she's tired of Munchie, and she wants to be with me. Now she's *really* 'bout to sit here and marry this bitch?"

"Calm down, Shanice." I wanted to tell her, "This shit ain't even a real wedding. What the hell are you so mad for?" But I minced my words. Everybody was looking. You could hear a spider spin a web.

"You not about to fuck up my wedding, Shanice," Munchie said, stepping away from the makeshift altar. Shanice had her sock, but there wasn't any rice in it. It was a lock, and she swung it on Munchie as soon as she got too close to her. Blood flew from Munchie's nose. The peaceful wedding turned into bloody mayhem.

Chapter 21

ESHE

"Ain't no smile on my face . . . I don't see nothing funny . . . if you really wanna feel me . . . take me to the money!" I kept trying to find the right line for my next bar, but I didn't quite like the way it sounded. I spent a lot of time writing music. I loved rap, and when I was younger, I used to perform at local venues. I got so caught up in my businesses, that I put my passion for music to the side. But now that I had years of downtime, I started to pick my pen up again. It was cool because Milla and Sun-Solé would drop a verse or two occasionally, and we'd have our own private ciphers.

We had so much in common. I was really starting to love those chicks, and I felt closer to them than some of my friends at home. When you do time with someone, you get to know them in a way that you'll never get to know other people unless you live with them. You get to see how they maneuver on a daily basis in different types of circumstances.

My thoughts were interrupted by mail call. We stood in front of the officer's station like cattle. Actually, we were more like sheep, and when our names got called, it was a sign that we would not be slaughtered today. Our names getting called at mail call was the ultimate sign that somebody, somewhere, had thought enough about us to pick up a pen and paper, or purchase a card to let us know that we were not forgotten. It was the most anticipatory time of the day. Like a battery charge helping you get through the next twenty-four hours.

"Eshe Haller!" the guard screamed out.

"Here!" I said as I shouldered my way through the crowd to get my mail.

"Hold up, you got about two more." He went through the stack and handed the mail to me.

"Milla Davison!"

"Here!" she said, then grabbed her mail and went off to her room. I went to mine. I was sure Sun-Solé would get mail too. That husband of hers, H, always wrote her every single day. A few minutes later, Milla was in my room.

"Guess what, Eshe? They moved KG to Atlanta USP."

"Are you serious? That's crazy." She then showed me the return address of her letter. Sure enough, it was Atlanta USP. That was a little spooky, being that there were tens of federal prisons around the country.

What were the odds of my codefendants, Marcellus and Jerry, Sun-Sole's husband, H, and now King-G too, all being at the same spot together? It was crazy, but a good crazy nonetheless. King-G just got moved there after getting sentenced to life. The whole thought of that was too much to bear for any of us. King-G was a household name, like Drake, Future, Jadakiss, or Jay-Z. They were black

America's distant family linked through the blood of media.

Milla didn't have approval to correspond with him, so I would now drop a scribe from her to King-G, with my letter to Marcellus or Jerry. This way, he'd know that Milla had him on her mind.

Not long after KG got there, the guards got scared. Marcellus explained in his letter that KG was placed in the hole because they felt he had too much influence over other inmates. They did that sometimes with high-profile cases. It was foul. The system was killing us in more than one way. In the streets and on top of that, off of rumors (a.k.a. conspiracy charges). When I opened Jerry's letter, I couldn't believe what he was telling me:

Boss Lady,

Remember what I used to do working on Seven Mile? Before I met you and I was working out da crib? Opportunity. The vice principal at my job is into the same thing I used to love being into. He's about to move close to that spot, sis. He fucks with your girl Sun-Solé's boy. They were making some heavy moves, but while in the process of making things happen, the VP got transferred to Boss. Tell Boss to get with him quick when he comes that way. He already knows who Boss is, and he owes me

*a favor. Nothing is off limits, sis, so work
your magic!*

Love,

Your Brother for Life,

Jerry

Once I deciphered what he was saying, it basically meant
that the assistant warden at his prison was about to or had
just transferred here to this prison, and he's a crook. When
Jerry talked about his "old job," he's talking about when he
used to move weight back in the day. This assistant warden
coming here was into bringing drugs into the prison. I had
to talk to my sisters about what we could do with this cat
because I could smell opportunity in the air. I met with
Milla and Sun-Solé in the dining hall to talk about it.

"Check this out, ladies. We've been here for over a
year now. I don't know about y'all, but I don't have shit
anymore. The Feds took everything from us, and we're
moving on fumes right now. Milla, KG is fighting a life
sentence, and Sun-Solé, H is doing some serious numbers.
And my brothers and I are all facing this bullshit murder
charge. If we're going to be here, we might as well make it
work for us."

"I feel you, Eshe. So what you talkin' 'bout? I've had
a few ideas myself that I've been playing with in my head."

"I second that," Sun-Solé added. "You already know I
been thinking of some ways to get shit crackin'. I leave first

to go home before either of you, so this is important right here."

"Okay. Well, good that we're all on the same page. So look . . . all of the men in our lives are locked up together. I got some information today from Jerry telling me that the dude coming here as the assistant warden is down for whatever. They've been moving dope through the prison in ATL."

"That's cool and all, but I am not about to get no drug charge," Sun-Solé said. "That's not my hustle."

"Definitely not worth it," Milla added.

"Who said anything about drugs? There are other things we can get him to do for us, that will help us make money but has nothing to do with drugs. We just have to think outside the box. Drugs messed up our people enough. I want no parts of that either. So drugs are out of the question," Eshe said.

"So what else can we do? What other kind of moves can we make that will help us get these moneybags?" Sun-Solé inquired.

"I got it! I got it, y'all!" Milla said excitedly.

"What?" Sun-Solé and I said in unison.

"Pink Panther Records!"

"What the hell is that, Milla? Pink Panther Records? I don't get it."

"We can start a record label from prison. Let's get the assistant warden to bring us studio equipment. I'm talkin' 'bout soundboards, microphones, drum kits, an Apple computer—the whole nine."

"Are you serious?" Sun-Solé asked.

"I'm dead serious," Milla said. That idea was the best thing I've heard so far. Music and money, the two things I breathed. It sounded almost too good to be true.

"So, hold up a minute. Where would we put this . . . studio?" I asked.

"In the chapel. Check this out . . . They have a room in the back of the chapel where they store all these CDs, microphones, and fifty-year-old records that the church uses. We can clear that room out and put the studio in there. We can drop some hot music from federal prison and put it out for the world. Think about it," Milla said. "I got some studio engineering background."

"Me too," Sun-Solé added. "H used to stay in the studio. So I picked up a li'l somethin' too."

"You do have a point, Milla. I mean, at the end of the day, chicks like us are rare. How many females you know that were making millions, living the life we lived, and doing what we do? Not too many. And not only that, we did it on our own. We weren't driving our boyfriends' cars, or sitting at home letting dudes take care of us. We're all bosses," I said proudly.

"No question! So from this day forward, not only do we have Pink Panther Records, we da Pink Panther Clique!"

Chapter 22

MILLA

The call-out sheets were given out last night, listing any place that any inmate had to be and what time they had to be there. I had two call-outs today. The first one was to the dentist. I put in a request to see the dentist a minute ago because of a toothache, and it is only now, eight months later, that I am being seen for it. There were no words to describe the deficiencies of federal prison.

My second call-out was to see the assistant warden, Mr. Pulls, at noon. As soon as the clock struck twelve, I was sitting outside his office. Then to my surprise, Eshe came along and sat beside me. "Girl, what are you doing here?" I asked.

"Shit, I don't know. I was on the call-out."

"Me too!" We were speaking in soft whispers. What were the odds of him calling us both at the same time?

"Come in, ladies," he yelled from behind closed doors.

We walked in, and I immediately noticed the air reeked of cheap cologne and cigarette smoke. He knew good and well he wasn't supposed to be smoking in a federal building. But obviously, this man didn't care about rules or laws, which was good for us. The office was plush. Looked more like a congressman's office to me.

"Hello, sir," I said. Eshe nodded. She had no respect for authority whatsoever and didn't try to hide it either. I didn't necessarily see these people as authoritative figures myself, but more so, I knew how to be an actress in order to get what I wanted.

"Have a seat," he said, spreading his arms. He was white, partially bald, but in pretty good shape. Probably no older than fifty.

"Thank you! I wanted to talk to you briefly about some things. I know you know my boyfriend. His name is—" He cut me off.

"King-G. Yes, I am very fond of him."

"And you also know Eshe Haller," I said very matter-of-factly, since she didn't seem to want to engage in conversation with him.

"Yes, I've heard of Ms. Haller. I know Jerry and Marcellus. They're two interesting guys, I must say." Eshe nodded again. I kicked her under the table and gave her a slight nod.

"Okay, look, why am I on the call-out? I didn't request to speak with you. And honestly, I don't like being behind closed doors with the police for too long because I ain't trying to be mistaken for being a snitch. So, can we please get to the point of this meeting?"

I just shook my head. Leave it to Eshe.

"I like your fire, Ms. Haller. I do. Okay, let me get straight to it. I'm a man who likes to be as comfortable as possible. I'm sure you feel the same, like Jerry and

Marcellus. They spoke very highly of you. And obviously, you, Milla, are something special, if the world-famous King-G is crazy over you. Everything out of his mouth is Milla this and Milla that." That made my stomach instantly dance. I felt like I had butterflies swarming around my belly. The thought of KG thinking about me and speaking about me so often really warmed my heart. I just hoped that this was not the end for him, for us, and that he would eventually get out and not have to die in prison.

"That's nice to hear. We all know KG loves Milla. But right now, I wanna talk about money," Eshe said, interrupting my emotional moment. She knew I was an emotional creature, and I needed a second to process what this man just told me. But she didn't wait for my recovery. She jumped right in, like she always does.

"I'm listening," he said.

"I already know you're looking to make some bread. That's the only reason you called us in here. Have you worked at a female prison before?"

"No. You ladies are the lucky winners."

"Okay, well, let me explain something to you. I know what you were doing at Atlanta USP. That won't work here. The drug use at female prisons is far lower than that at men's institutions. This is a different animal, and they snitch way too much. I don't know what it is about women in prison and talking to the police, but that's not a risk we're willing to take."

"I don't know what risk you're willing to take, nor do I care. I have two rules. The first is that my name stays out of anything you do. There will be no direct connection to me at all. If that happens, I go to great lengths to bring you down. And second, I need to make money. As long as we meet those two requirements, you ladies can do whatever you want. I wouldn't give a damn if you charged the ladies here a fee to use the television or charged rent for every room. As long as I get a cut, you have my blessing." He folded his hands together and sat all the way back in his plush leather chair.

"Well, here's what we need." I slid him a list of all the studio equipment. He looked at it, and then looked back up at me.

"Are you kidding me?" he said. And then he started laughing. However, he laughed by himself because Eshe and I just stared at him. Then he stopped. "Oh, you're serious? You've gotta be kidding me."

"We've got $5,000 we're working with. That's it. We pooled our money together. Get all this stuff. I don't care if it's used, as long as it works. You can keep whatever you don't spend, and we'll go from there."

"This is play money, ladies. I thought you all were big time," he said sarcastically.

"We'll show you who we are; just keep your word and handle this."

We told him where to go pick up the money. It took about two weeks, but we were able to get the chapel to approve the equipment, under the guise of the prison choir recording music for charity. So we had to let the chapel use the studio as well. But it didn't matter. Whenever they weren't, we were using it on the low. The assistant warden worked his magic and got us on the cleaning crew for the chapel without supervision. That was our daily studio time.

I had unlimited connections in the music industry. Thanks to my baby KG, I was able to get one of the hottest producers to send in some beats just on the strength of his name. And when we laid our first track, I knew we were on to something. Me, Eshe, and Sun-Solé. We had a story to tell. And it wasn't made up bullshit; everything we spoke about was real. All of us had flow. The challenge was now getting our music out there without prison officials knowing. I hadn't got that far yet, but I'd figure something out. That's what I did . . . I figured things out.

Then it hit me. I wrote King-G and told him to spit a verse over the phone to Biggie's "One More Chance," so we could know the tempo and pick the right track to lay it down on. Under my label, Pink Panther Records, I was going to release a single for my man while he was locked up. People were going to go crazy if we pulled this off. And behind him, the Pink Panther Clique would drop a follow-up hit. Well, I hoped it would be a hit. None of us had ever gone this far with music, but we were sure as hell going to try. We'd record as much material as possible, so if they took the studio away, we'd already have enough music done to keep us relevant. I had 100 percent faith in the plan. Creativity should never go to waste, and I looked forward to making sure ours didn't. I only hoped we made some money. Because if not, I was sure Mr. Pulls would make good on his threat to take us down.

Chapter 23

SUNNY-SOLÉ

Prison was a waste of time. It was full of drama and even worse, the staff was miserable. A girl who lived a few cubes down from me just found out this morning that her son shot himself. He had severe mental illness. As a matter of fact, the reason she was here was because she robbed a bank in order to raise money for his medication. She couldn't afford it. It didn't make bank robbery okay, but it sure made you understand the actions of a desperate mother. Everybody had a story. Everybody had a breaking point. That one thing in their life that made them say, "fuck it." I felt bad for her. Ms. Glads, we called her, received thirty-four years for robbery, and she never even had a weapon. She only passed a note to the bank teller. Now her son was dead, and she was not handling it well.

Thank goodness we could go to the studio and let off some steam. I had to get away from all the sadness in the unit. I had a lot to say in the booth. Even if nothing came from the music we did, it was therapeutic. There was nothing like speaking my mind, especially over a fire beat.

"I don't understand why everybody's in such an uproar. I lost my mother, father, and my brother since I been down. People die. It's part of life," Mona said. She was a petite Indian girl who swore she was black.

"We know people die, but damn, have a heart," I responded.

"Whatever, Sun-Solé! Bitches are too dramatic," Mona, my new bunkie, said. I didn't like her. She was nothing like Munchie. Munchie was in the hole after that whole wedding fight broke out. I hoped that she could come and reclaim the room once she got out. I couldn't stand this new chick. The wedding was a disaster; it ended up turning into a big brawl and getting us banned from being on the yard without supervision for a while. I managed to stay out of the miniwar, thank goodness. I only fought if I had to, and that situation didn't seem worthy of my time or energy. Couples, they kept some shit going in this bitch. Turns out, messing with females could be worse than dealing with men. I just wanted to do my time and go home. My thoughts were interrupted by the loudspeaker.

"Inmate Sun-Solé Williamson. . . Sun-Solé Williamson, report to the officer's station." What the hell did they want now? I got off my bunk and headed toward the officer's station.

"What's up?" I asked the officer.

"The warden wants to see you."

"Me? For what?"

"I don't know. That's not my job." The bitch always had to say something sarcastic.

I walked to the warden's office and waited in the lobby. "Can I help you?" his secretary asked, looking me up and down. She used to be a regular corrections officer, but somehow, she got a promotion.

"I was told to come over here to see the warden."

"Any call-outs for the warden, I handle that. And I never called for you. He doesn't see inmates in his office."

"Okay . . . well, I was told to come down here. Shit, what if I got immediate release? I'm going to wait for him."

"No, you're going to leave and go back up to your unit. If you don't, I'll write you an incident report. What makes you so special that the warden wants to see you?"

"An incident report?"

"Yes, are you deaf, inmate?"

"I'm not going through this. A'ight, lady. I'm out!" I got up to leave because I knew my temper, and I'd be in the hole with another charge in a minute if that bitch said the wrong thing to me. Then the warden walked in just as I was leaving.

"Mrs. Williamson?" he said. "Where are you going?"

"Back to my unit."

"Didn't they tell you I called for you?" he asked, puzzled. I looked at his secretary, Ms. Schitz.

"Ms. Schitz told me if I didn't leave, she was going to write me up. She was real nasty," I said, rolling my eyes.

"Is this true, Ms. Schitz?" he asked.

"Well, I mean, umm, she came in here demanding to see you, and I didn't know anything about it. So I told her to go back to her unit."

"She didn't say it that way," I corrected. The bitch was trying to talk all nice and sweet now.

"I apologize, Ms. Williamson. Please, my office," he said, nodding in the direction of his office. "And you, Schitz, when she leaves, come see me," he said sternly. I wanted to give her the finger, but I knew he would handle it. Something about his character assured me that he would.

"So . . . Ms. Williamson, how are you today?"

"I'm good. So what's this about?" I asked, wanting to get straight to the point.

"It's about inmate Gaines. You know, you all refer to her as Prego. She's about seven or so months pregnant right now. How is your rapport with her?"

"I mean, we're cool. Why?"

"I've gotten a few kites from some of the other women in your unit complaining about some inappropriate behavior between her and Lieutenant Longwood. I've called several other women to see if there is any truth to this." *Does this muthafucka think I'm a snitch? He got me fucked up if he does.*

"Nah, I don't know nothing about that. Can I go now?" He smiled.

"I admire you, Ms. Williamson. I do. I've kept my eye on you." He was definitely a nice-looking man, and I purposely avoided looking him in the eyes. "I see how you move around here. I respect it. But my job is to avoid any lawsuits, and if we have a pregnant woman being taken advantage of in any way, I need to know about it. I run a clean prison. First, as a warden, and also as a man and a father. It's my personal responsibility."

"Well, I haven't seen anything inappropriate. But if I do, I'll let you know."

"Thank you! You can go now."

That was extremely weird. First of all, investigations into officers were handled by the SIS department. Not the warden. Second, there was just something about the look on his face that didn't sit right with me. And I would definitely figure out what the hell was going on.

"Prego!" I called out. She was sitting in the television room watching a movie.

"What's up?" she said, wobbling over to me.

"Listen, I'm telling you something, and you better not say shit. I don't know what the hell is going on with you and Lieutenant Longwood, but the warden has been asking questions. I'm not getting all in your business, but just be careful."

"What kind of questions?" she asked nervously.

"He just wanted to know if there was anything inappropriate going on with you and the lieutenant. I told him no. Somebody is telling him stuff. So just be on point."

"There's nothing to be on point about. I mean, I can tell he likes me, but the lieutenant is cool." She couldn't lie to me. I saw them fucking with my own eyes. And what type of man fucks a pregnant girl? She came into the prison pregnant, and it was just disgusting to me for one man to be nutting on another man's baby. But whatever. To each his own. It wasn't my business.

"Count time!" the guard yelled out. I went back to my bed and stood in front of it for the 4:00 p.m. count. I'd been counted five times a day every single day since I got here. It was depressing. We were like cattle. It usually took about five minutes to clear count. But rather than yell "count," they hollered, "recount!" They counted us again. After the third time, they told us to take out our identification cards. Something wasn't right. What the hell was going on? They walked up to each of us and matched our IDs with our bed numbers.

Lieutenant Longwood and the captain ran into the unit and whispered to the unit officer. "It's confirmed. Glads is missing. We think she escaped. Lock the place down now!"

Chapter 24

ESHE

We'd been on lockdown for an entire week, and finally, just a few minutes ago, the restricted movement was lifted. It was horrible. First, the U.S. Marshals came in and put yellow crime scene tape around Ms. Glad's room. We didn't know what that meant. We just knew that we were suffering because of it. Second, there was a mandatory lockdown, and we were on emergency protocol. Every count was a census count, and there were too many guards on each unit. It was a pain in the ass.

We didn't shower for days, so most of us smelled like old onions. We didn't have bathrooms in our cubes because we weren't in cells. They just locked the shower room and had controlled bathroom movements. As the days went on, the smell in the unit turned into more like rotten sewage. We didn't get to eat in the dining hall. We had flight meals, which were box lunches that they gave out on the plane when you flew on Con-Air, the airline they used to transport prisoners. Each prison had stockpiles of old flight meals for emergency purposes. It usually consisted of either melted peanut butter that was more like peanut oil, or old cheese and "mystery" meat, with some pretzels and a pack of poison known as prison Kool-Aid. Everybody knew: don't drink the Kool-Aid!

Not long after we were released from lockdown, information started to flood the unit about what happened. Of course, my girl Sun-Solé had the inside scoop. She came running over to my room in her robe.

"Where's Milla?"

"She's on line for the shower. Same place I'm going, and your ass needs to be going too."

"I am. Why you think I got this robe on? I just had to tell you what's going on. Rumor has it that they found Ms. Glads, and she's . . . dead!" My hands covered my mouth.

"You're kidding me. Oh my God!"

"Her son's death was just too much for her. They say she had made it to the mountains about three miles from here. And she passed out because she didn't have her insulin. They said a black bear got her up in them mountains because the way her body was mutilated was horrific. They say it looked gruesome."

"That is unacceptable. She had all the signs. They wouldn't let her go to her son's funeral. She didn't have money to use the phone; she was a keg of gunpowder, and his death lit the match. Sad. And these people should be liable in some way. She wasn't well." Once Sun-Solé had the drop on something, it was usually accurate. We jumped on the shower line and informed Milla.

"How sure are you about this?" Milla asked Sun-Solé.

"I'm 100 percent positive. I heard it from the warden myself. I saw the preliminary death certificate. It said she escaped by death."

"Escaped by death?"

"Yes, if any of us die before our sentence is up, our death certificates says 'escaped by death.' How sick is that?"

"I don't believe that."

"I'm telling you, I saw it myself."

"Wait a minute. How did you see it? How did you . . . When did you see him? We've been on lockdown for days."

"He called me out yesterday," she said matter-of-factly.

"I don't know if H would appreciate the warden coming to see his queen so often."

"Girl, bye! Ain't nobody thinking about that man. I just communicate with him so we stay on top of everything going on around here."

"Well, I think he likes you."

"And if he does, better for us. But I wasn't the only one he came to see. He also checked on Prego to make sure that she was being properly cared for while we were on lock. He's not a bad dude," Sun-Solé said.

"Not bad at all, with his fine self. But he sure takes a lot of interest in her too," I added.

"Maybe he's just a real man who cares about a pregnant woman," Milla said. Milla always tried to see the good in a person. Regardless of their position.

"Or maybe he knows that she's fucking Lieutenant Longwood," I said.

"Oh, he definitely suspects it, but he has no proof," Sun-Solé informed. "He asked me if I'd heard anything and told me how he doesn't tolerate none of that shit in his prison."

"Well, now that we're out, after we get freshened up, let's see if we can head down to the studio. I did some writing while we were on lock, and I'm tired of talking about the warden."

Kiera Johnson lived two cubes down from me. She was a nice girl but got caught up in a drug conspiracy that had nothing to do with her. Her boyfriend was a big supplier from Chicago. And when he got charged, they wanted her to snitch on him. She refused, so she got hit with ten years. She was coming up toward the end of her sentence. But for some reason, she didn't look happy to be getting ready to go home. She seemed stressed out. I ran into her at the law library, and I sat down next to her.

"Kiera, what's up? You been looking down, girl. Everything okay?"

"Not really. After all these years, the end is the hardest. They're only giving me two months halfway house. And as you know, without halfway house time, we get stuck in prison doing almost all of our time here. I got a ten-year sentence, and I feel like I deserve a year halfway house time."

"What about the Second Chance Act? Isn't that legally binding them to give you up to eighteen months? One year halfway house and six months home confinement?"

"Nothing binds them. They do what they want. I don't have any place to go. I don't have any money, no job lined up. I've been gone for eight years. I had a couple fights and lost my good time. But that has nothing to do with halfway house time. I'm just so frustrated. They're gonna let me out of here and expect me to catch up with the world in just sixty days? That's not even realistic."

"What about Becky Wickers? The white girl from Massachusetts? She only had a two-year sentence, but I hear she's getting eleven months' halfway house. Let's ask her what she did," I suggested.

The two of us left the library to go find Becky. After good-time and almost a year halfway house, Becky would only end up doing ten months. I don't see how that was fair. Halfway houses were for people who needed help to get readjusted and reacclimated back into society. Why would a girl who just came to prison take up space, blocking other inmates who really needed that help? It just didn't make any sense.

We found Becky in the recreation room, running on the treadmill and reading a magazine. She was a petite white girl with long, blond hair and large breasts. She looked like a typical hostess at Hooters.

"Becky, can we holler at you for a minute?" I asked. She looked me up and down, and then smiled. She was one of those inmates everybody wanted to stay away from. Always complaining about her time. It was funny how short-timers always cried, and us chicks with the longer sentences took it like Gs. We realized nothing came from crying about water under the bridge. We fought our cases, but we didn't let the time do us.

"So what's up?" Becky said, stepping off the treadmill and drying herself off with an institutional brown towel.

"I'm just curious, and you don't have to answer me if you don't want to, but how did you get almost a year halfway house with such a short sentence?"

"I didn't ask for it. They offered it to me. I don't know."

"Who's your counselor?" I asked. Kiera stood there listening.

"Ms. Cheiders."

"Okay, thanks," I said to Becky. I pulled Kiera to the side. "Come on, let's go to her open house."

"I really don't want to. Ms. Cheiders used to be an officer before you got here, and she's a real bitch. She's racist, she's mean, and she hates her job. I'll just deal with the two months."

"No, fuck that. We don't get far in life by being complacent and laying down. Go explain your case and make sure that they do right by you. You've done too much time to be slighted at the end. I'll help you if you're willing to help yourself." I finally got Kiera to agree.

We arrived at Ms. Cheiders's office during her open house hours. I told Kiera I couldn't go in there with her, but I equipped her with what she needed to say. I also pulled policy so she could quote it and make sure they didn't do her wrong.

Kiera came out of there crying. I instantly felt bad for putting her in this position to ask this woman for anything.

"Just forget it, Eshe. She did everything but laugh in my face."

"We'll write her up. Don't get discouraged." We started walking back toward the unit, and we ran into Becky.

"How did it go?" she asked, now drying her blond hair with the same towel from the rec.

"It didn't go. She's a bitch. I don't know how you got her to give you all that time, but that shit isn't fair. What's good for one is good for all. Especially somebody who's done five times the amount of time you've done. Nothing against you, but I'm just saying; these people are racist."

Becky pulled the two us, Kiera and me, over to the corner and talked in a hushed tone. "Look, if you want a year halfway house, I can make it happen. Don't say shit about this, but come up with $20,000, and she'll do it."

"You trippin', girl. And get caught up in some bribing-an-officer shit? Nah!" Kiera said.

"You're not listening, girl. How do you think I got my halfway house time? Money talks and bullshit walks!" Becky assured.

I couldn't believe what I was hearing. Twenty thousand dollars for halfway house time? Something the law already made provisions for? Man, this was exploitation at its finest, and I wasn't about to let this shit go down. Oh yeah, she was gonna give Kiera her proper due, and it wasn't gonna cost Kiera a dime either! Not as long as I had anything to do with it.

Chapter 25

MILLA

"What now?" I said out loud to myself, as I was awakened from my sleep. The captain and the assistant warden were on our unit screaming at the top of their lungs for us to get out of bed and report to the middle of the recreation floor. I looked at my watch. It was only six in the morning. This was too much. What the hell did they want?

"Okay, I am going to make this as clear as I possibly can. I do not tolerate cell phones in my prison!" the captain said. "I am going to give whoever has the shit a chance to fess up. Otherwise, *everybody* will be punished."

"Bullshit! Y'all stupid," one chick hollered.

"Fuck you! Do whatever. I'm going to sleep!" someone else screamed.

"That's not fair!" I said, adding my two cents. But, of course, with all the hollering, I was the one that he heard.

"Excuse me? You got something you wanna say?" Assistant Warden Pulls asked. He had a lot of nerve. I guess he needed to put on a show since he was the one who actually snuck us in all that studio equipment and was probably the one responsible for bringing in the same cell phones he's tripping about.

"Nah, I don't have anything to say . . . clown," I muttered.

"One by one, we will call each of you in. Do not leave this area." While they questioned us, they searched our units, literally tearing the place apart. Everybody was pissed. I mean, we knew we were in prison, but it was such an invasion of privacy.

Prego wobbled over to me. "Hey, Milla. Sun-Solé was looking for you. She's over by the phones."

"Girl, you're getting so big. Shouldn't you be delivering soon?"

"Yeah. Soon."

"What's your due date?" I asked her.

"Oh damn. Hold up. I gotta use the bathroom," she said and walked away. I noticed that about her. Every single time I asked her, or anybody else, for that matter, about her due date, she found a way to either change the topic or walk away. It was weird. We all knew she was pregnant; she was as big as a house, and she was coming up on at least eight months now. I didn't understand.

It was looking like being pregnant here was the way to go. Prego had a double mattress; she got double food portions, and she supposedly went to the doctor's office every week, even though my girls and I were all pretty sure that she was going with Longwood for long nights. I wasn't hating on the sister, but damn, it was a messed up situation. Maybe her husband abandoned her. He never came to visit her, so maybe there's more to what appeared in front of the naked eye. Who am I to judge? It's not my business anyway. I have bigger issues to deal with. My man is dealing with a life sentence, and I couldn't front like that didn't bother me.

I checked myself once again for referring to him as my man. He was, but this situation deaded all of that. I had to accept it and move on. My thoughts were interrupted by the guard calling out my name.

"Again . . . Inmate Davison, report to the unit officer." What the hell did they want with me? I spotted Sun-Solé and Eshe chillin' by the phones, and I waved at them. Eshe held up her hands to ask me what was up. I just shrugged. They were still in the middle of an intense search, so why they were calling me was a mystery.

"Whassup?" I asked the officer standing next to the captain overseeing the entire search.

"We just searched your room. What is this?"

"I don't know."

"Oh? You don't know? It was in your room, but you don't know?" the officer said.

"I have no idea."

"It looks like a cell phone charger."

"Well, if that's what it is, somebody put it there. And it wasn't me."

"I need a female officer to Unit B4," the officer said as he radio called someone to come to the unit. This was some bullshit. A few minutes later, two female officers arrived.

"What you need?" Officer Hayts asked him.

Great, the worst of the worst. I couldn't stand her. The weave thief.

"I need you to strip this one out and make sure she's not hiding anything."

"My pleasure," she said, looking at me. Still rocking that same old weave. It took everything in me to keep from laughing.

"Come with me, Milla Davison." She took me to a private strip out room in a part of the prison I had never been to before. "I knew you would be trouble. Clothes off," she said. I ignored her comments and began stripping down until I was butt-ass naked.

"Pass me your socks . . . now your pants." She checked every pocket and crevice. "Now give me your shoes." I was standing on the cold-ass floor, barefoot. All I kept thinking about was getting in the shower once I left this stankin'-ass room. She checked the inside of my shoes. "Okay, now pass me your panties." She ran her gloved hand across the crotch of my underwear, and then placed them with my other clothes on a dirty, dusty table. "Now, bend at the waist, and squat. Cough three times." I did as I was told. "Now get dressed."

I put my pants back on, no panties. I would never put those on again. They'd been in her hands and on a dirty table. "Can I go now?" I asked once I was dressed.

"What do you think you're doing?"

"What's the problem?" I asked, cocking my head to the side and frowning.

"You didn't put your panties on. You put them in the trash." She went to the trash can and pulled them out, passing them to me. "Put them on."

"No! They're contaminated now. You touched them; you laid them on a dirty table, and now they are in the garbage."

"I don't care. What does BOP policy state? Inmates are to wear underwear at all times. So, you're not leaving this room until you put them panties on."

"Lady, you got me fucked up! I'm not putting them panties on. As a matter of fact, call the lieutenant." She folded her arms in protest. I walked over to the door and tried to open it, but it was locked. Hayts smiled. Oh, hell, no. I wasn't trying to get any new charges, but I damn surely would fight this bitch in this room, if she didn't let me up out of here.

"I got all day," she said.

"Yo, what is your issue? You've had a problem since day one."

"No, *you're* the problem, Inmate! Don't you know you're a prisoner? You and your li'l homegirls walk around here like y'all own the world. You ain't shit but a damn criminal."

"First of all, you don't know me. You don't know anything about me. I'm sorry that my success is such a threat to you. You can call me inmate, prisoner, or whatever you want. But that's just a matter of opinion. Nothing you say can hurt me, lady. Now, let me out of this room before we have a problem." I said it as calmly as I could.

"Is that a threat, Inmate?" she screamed at the top of her lungs. "Turn around, turn around and put your hands behind your back, you little bitch!" *Yo, this chick is out of her mind.* "You think you can challenge me!" she screamed so loud you would have thought I was in the next room, not just two feet in front of her. "As long as you are here, you are only—" Suddenly she stopped talking. She grabbed her chest. Then she let out a piercing scream, followed by the bending of her knees.

"Yo! Hayts! You all right?"

"Mmm . . . ahh, I can't. I can't breathe!" Then she hit the floor. Her eyes were open, but she was incoherent.

Oh my God! Is this bitch having a heart attack?

I didn't know what to do. I picked up her radio. I hit the button on the side. "Emergency! Emergency! A guard is down."

"Who is this?" a male voice said over the radio.

"Ummm, I'm Jamila Davison #59253-053."

"What? An inmate? Where the hell are you?"

"I don't know, in one of the strip rooms. The door is locked."

"Code Red. We've got a hostage situation. Hostage situation in progress."

Oh, hell, no! That is not what's going on. I added my own code red.

"That is false. I repeat: that is false. The officer took . . ." The radio did a few beeps, and then cut off in the middle of me talking. The battery died. This was crazy. I started banging on the door. "Help! Help!" Officer Hayts was on the floor, now unconscious. *Oh shit!* I grabbed her keys from her belt. There were so many of them, I didn't know which one would work. It wasn't until I got to the fifth key that I was able to get the door open.

I dragged her by her feet out of the room and into the hallway. There was a defibrillator machine on the wall. She had no pulse. I didn't even think about it; I just went into action, opened up her shirt, and hit the defibrillator. Her entire body jerked. I listened to her chest. Still nothing. No pulse. I did it again. Nothing. This shit didn't work.

When I was younger, I was trained in CPR. I tried that: "One, two, three, four," then I blew in her mouth. Nothing. I did it again, but before I could give her my next breath, officers swarmed the hall and grabbed me off of her. Before I knew it, I was being thrown up against the wall violently, and my arms were twisted behind my back.

"You think you can hurt one of us? You think?!" he screamed. Tears formed in my eyes.

"No! No! I was trying to help!" Suddenly, Hayts began to cough. She was trying to say something.

"She . . . She . . . saved . . ."

"Quiet, don't talk. Don't talk. The paramedics are on their way." They dragged me to the hole and literally tossed me in. I hadn't even done anything. Now I was being held for taking an officer hostage.

Now, ain't that a bitch!

Chapter 26

SUNNY-SOLÉ

I can't believe they've got my girl held up on these crazy-ass charges. Kidnapping? That doesn't even make any sense. Maybe I would do some shit like that, but not Milla. That one officer had it out for her. For all of us. They hadn't even found any cell phones. Somebody tried to set Milla up. She doesn't have a phone; neither does anyone that I know. And my ears are always to these prison streets. I knew most of what was going on around here. But this . . . I didn't like. However, I had a hunch about what was up, and I was going to find out.

Finally, we were allowed to go back to our rooms.

"They still haven't brought her back yet?" Eshe asked, stepping up to my doorway.

"No. And I'm pissed. I'm going to talk to the assistant warden. He has to help her. She didn't do anything."

"Well, it won't hurt to try. I don't really like him. Something about him is off. But go and try your luck, sis." That's exactly what I planned to do. I went to the office of Assistant Warden Pulls, demanding to talk to him. He told his secretary to let me in. He was sitting behind his desk talking on the phone. When he saw me, he waved his pointer finger, letting me know he was almost done. When he hung up, I skipped all the pleasantries.

"Why is my friend Jamila Davison sitting in solitary confinement with pending kidnapping and hostage charges? She didn't take that lady to that room. And I know she didn't hurt her. This doesn't make any sense." My voice was sharp and clear. There was no submissive nature to my tone. I looked him dead in the eyes and demanded answers.

"We'll leave that to the officer to say what happened. She's in recovery right now after having triple bypass surgery. Once she comes to, let's hope she can vouch for your friend."

"And what if she can't?" I said, now placing my hands on my hips.

"Looks like we'll have to reevaluate our little agreement."

"First of all—" I said in an attempt to talk, but he cut me off in midsentence.

"No! Let me explain something to *you*." He got up and closed the door. "I am a businessman. I did what you ladies asked. I got you that stupid studio, and so far, I haven't made a dime. What the hell is the point? I don't play games, but I did you a favor. I've gained nothing from my risks."

"If I find out you set her up!" I said, ignoring him.

"What? If you find out *what?*" he asked, throwing his hands up.

"So you did!" I blurted, after staring at him briefly. I could read a lie a mile away. The revelation just came to me. "So you put that phone charger in her property so you could pressure us to make you some money?"

"Bravo, Williamson. Bravo! Yes! Yes, I did. And I'm telling you right now, you've got one month! Just one month, and she will be shipped out of here. I better start making some money. You see, I can't go down without you going down as well. So I'm not worried about retaliation."

"You're a real asshole," I said, rolling my eyes and folding my arms across my chest.

"I've been called worse." He sat back and relaxed in his chair.

I humbled myself, realizing the position we were in. "Okay, look . . . at least let her out every day to come to the studio so we can make some things happen. Just three hours a day. We can do a lot. We'll have some money for you in a month."

"You better. Or you can say good-bye to your friend . . . for a very long time."

I left his office feeling defeated. I didn't like anyone holding shit over my head, but that is exactly what's happening. A big pile of shit was dangling above us like a dark cloud. I ran to tell Eshe about this situation. She couldn't believe he would do that to us at first. But then, she thought about it some more.

"That is foul, yo. But life is a chess game, and he's playing chess with us. We gotta respect the situation. We didn't want to get involved in the drug game, which would have been the most lucrative way to make them moneybags. We wanted to stay as clean as possible. But clean money is slow money. So because of that, we took a different type of risk. Music. I love music. But like I said, it's what we love, not necessarily something that makes overnight money. So we have to find a way to hold up our end of the bargain," Eshe said.

"I feel you, Eshe. But that is no excuse for him to set Milla up like that. Hell, no!"

"Yeah, he went in a foul direction in trying to force our hand, but it worked. He saw an opportunity, and he exploited it. Unfortunately, he's got one point, and he's right—he's not making money. And neither are we. So now the pressure is on, and we gotta get our sister out of this situation and get some bread at the same time. We gotta get this situation under control."

We dapped on it. The two of us went to the studio and got to work. Every day we were working hard. We laid down a few tracks. The first one we did was called: "BBS (Boss Bitch Shit)." It was dope. The only verse missing was Milla's, and we couldn't wait to let her hear it. Then the idea hit me. "Eshe, I'm sending a kite to King-G. Express mail. I'll send it with Melissa who goes home tomorrow. She can go to the post office and overnight it."

Melissa kept her word. She sent the letter to King-G.

The next evening I made some phone calls, and I found out that King-G already got my letter and did what I asked. I couldn't believe it. It took an extra day, but once Eshe saw what I was able to pull off, she damn near lifted me off the ground she was so excited. "Sun-Solé, this is dope! Dope, ma!" I couldn't believe it. We did it! Only thing missing was our sis.

Finally, Assistant Warden Pulls kept his promise. He let Milla out of the hole to come to the studio. Of course, all the other staff just thought she was being allowed to come to church. We felt bad for Milla. Everybody was looking at her like she was some cop-kidnapping maniac. But the people who had the opportunity to bond with her over what was now almost a year knew that this wasn't true. We tried to cheer her up by telling her that the officer was still in the hospital and in recovery from her surgery, and hopefully, she could clear her name.

Milla nodded and somberly joined us in the booth. But it wasn't until she heard the track that she went crazy. "I got a surprise for you," I said.

"Am I getting out of here tonight?" Milla joked. I was happy that she was making an attempt to keep her own spirits high. That's why I loved my sis.

"Nah, I got something better. Listen to this." The track came on and began to play:

♫ *Boss Boss Boss chicks/Boss Boss Boss chicks/Moneybags tight*

We be on dat Boss shit/ Boss Boss Boss chicks . . . ♫

Milla's head bopped in approval as the beat banged. Then the verse dropped that blew her away!

♫ *Chanel draped, shorty gotta bad bad bad shape/A mill on her wrist/I wouldn't trade her for no other chick/Everything she do mamí gotta do it large/And she a boss boss bitch/Rode wid me on da charge/I ain't put a diamond on her finger/I kept one on every finger/When she walk up out a room her sexy image always linger . . .* ♫

I looked up at Milla to see tears falling down her cheeks. King-G had laid this verse for her over the phone. Then he had his producers send it to us already mixed and laid down on our song. Milla jumped on the track and killed it. It was a wrap. We had our first real banger, made and recorded from prison. Now it was time to release the track. Pink Panther Records was definitely in the building. Now, the only thing left to do was let the world know about it.

Chapter 27

ESHE

"Aisha! Aisha!" I heard someone screaming out my name. Nobody ever called my name like that. The police either called me Haller, my last name, or they called me Eshe like everybody else. So who the hell was calling out my government name like that? I looked around, and I saw it was Kiera. I gave her a look, but the smile on her face was not going anywhere. Slowly, I climbed down from my bunk.

"What's up, girl?"

"Aisha! That's what they're saying on the radio. Aisha, Jamila, Sun-Solé, and King-G. Those are the names on every radio station right now. Listen!" She passed me her radio. Our song was playing!

"Oh shit! Sun-Solé! Sun-Solé!" Now I was screaming, running down the unit to Sun-Solé's room. She wasn't in her room. It was eight in the morning. Where the hell was she? I couldn't believe that we were on the radio. I called my family, and they too were screaming in the phone. My younger sister was the most excited.

"Eshe, yo, y'all killing the blogs, Instagram, Snapchat, Facebook, Twitter, everything."

"What are they saying?" I asked.

"Basically, that from prison, y'all released the hottest song of the year. They're going crazy over you and your girls, and, of course, King-G. Everybody is amazed. How the hell did y'all do it?"

"Girl, you can't ask me those kind of questions from prison."

"How can I buy it? Everybody wants to buy it, download it, something."

"I'll call you back and let you know. I'm on it today." I went to the officer's station, and when I knocked, I didn't wait to be told to come in. I just walked in. And there were six officers in there all standing around the radio listening to our song. They looked up at me in confusion.

"What?" I said. They were all quiet for a moment.

"So, I'm not even gonna ask how this happened. But trust and believe, y'all are going down. I don't know who y'all think you are," one of the officers said.

The young black guy didn't feel the same. "Man, fuck that. I think y'all are dope. That was hot. Congratulations!" he said.

"Thank you. I just need to get in touch with the assistant warden." The other officers ignored me. Haters. But the black dude, who looked to be no older than twenty-one or so, radio called him. I was told to make my way down to his office.

As I walked the administration area hallway, I had to pass the warden's office before getting to the assistant warden's office. The warden's door was slightly open. I walked past, but stopped in my tracks and backed up. I peered in and saw my girl Sun-Solé in there. What was she doing over here this early? The warden was in there, and they were having a good ol' conversation. I could hear bits and pieces.

"If only you weren't here," he said to her.

"What would happen?" Sun-Solé asked, seductively.

"Things I can't say."

"Well, I'm a married woman, so not much that you can't say would ever happen."

"Don't be so sure about that," he responded. "I could just stare at you all day long. You're beautiful. And your music, I don't know how y'all did that, but now I have to investigate. Why did you have to put me in this position?"

"Everything was done over the phone. There is nothing . . . absolutely nothing illegal about that." She said it slow and seductive sounding.

"You just think you can smile that pretty smile and I'll fold, huh?" the warden said. Sun-Solé let out a fake laugh. *That's my girl. Always keeping the status quo in our favor.* I walked down a few feet and knocked on the assistant warden's door.

"Come in." When I stepped in, he began clapping. "Bravo! Bravo! I see you girls did something constructive." Then he got serious. "But still, where's my money?" he asked in a whisper.

"It's coming. I can promise you that. It's coming. I just need my girl out of the hole. Please!"

"I can't do that. I still haven't gotten any money yet." I tossed all of the papers off his desk and leaned right up in his face.

"You are lucky! Lucky that I'm a prisoner and not in the street. I wouldn't hesitate to deal with you the way I deal with all my other problems." Jerry's face appeared in my head.

"Are you threatening me, young lady?" he said calmly. I didn't realize it right away, but I was breathing heavy, almost like a bull about to chase a red cape. I got a hold of myself and calmed down.

"You'll have your fucking money soon enough. I need to use your computer. And your phone." He laughed. But then his smile faded when he saw I was serious.

"For what?" he asked.

"You want your money, don't you?" He got up from his seat and closed his door all the way.

"Be quick," he said. I went behind his desk and picked up his cell phone. Milla had given me her good friend's number, so I called him. Jadakiss answered on the first ring. He was an exec on the KOMAR board. Big A-List artists were using KOMAR (Keeping and Owning Music and Rights). It was the new way artists were releasing music, and they were able to keep 90 percent of the proceeds. I told Jada I was sending the music to him via e-mail and for him to release the single on KOMAR.com. We made the single $1 to download. I gave him an e-mail address and told him to forward the contract ASAP.

I ended the call and checked my e-mail messages on his computer. The contract came over, and I printed it. Then I dropped the original in the mailbox and gave the okay via e-mail to instantly release the track on KOMAR. The assistant warden watched in awe as I handled my business. Before I logged off, I checked one other thing: how Mr. Pulls got his direct deposit. The BOP direct deposit page showed all of his existing banking information, so I memorized it. I walked toward the exit of his office. "Now, *that's* how boss bitches do shit!" I said. Then I left.

By 6:00 p.m., the song was available for international purchase. Every radio station was playing it, but it wasn't only about the song. It was the dynamics surrounding the song. There was so much controversy. Everybody wanted to know how the hell the song got released. We had enough material stored up now to get rid of the equipment. We knew that Region, the prison inspection folks, would be here any day to see if there was anything going on that shouldn't be.

By 5:00 p.m. the next day, all of the studio equipment was gone. By 4:00 p.m. the day after that, we'd sold over 100,000 downloads of the song on KOMAR. That was already $100,000 in gross sales we did in less than forty-eight hours! We were killing the radio, and the song was selling like crazy.

Milla was able to get out of the hole for her three hours. She called Jadakiss since he was part owner of KOMAR and asked if he would mind giving up an advance of $100,000 immediately, before KOMAR paid out its royalties, which would take another sixty days. He said he would see what he could do. Two days later, he agreed. It took him a week to make it happen, but he got it done.

When I used the assistant warden's computer, I got his bank wire information and we sent him $40,000, unbeknownst to him. We knew he hadn't a clue how much money we were making, so when he made his rounds we let him know we needed to talk. He told us to meet him in his office in five minutes.

"I'm going to have to move the equipment, ladies. Just for a little while. I've got Washington up my ass about this song. I can't believe I risked so much for so little." Nervously, he ran his hands through his hair.

"You don't have to move anything."

"Yeah, just leave all the evidence sitting around. You know, I thought you ladies were smart."

"We are. There's nothing to move. The equipment is gone."

"Gone?" he said surprised.

"Yes. Gone."

"Okay, well, good then," he said, realizing he'd underestimated us. But he hadn't seen anything yet.

"There is an offer on the table for you," Sun-Solé said to him. Neither she nor I cracked a smile.

"We already have a deal," he replied.

"Yeah, but this one is different. We can pay you four right away," I added.

"Four thousand? That's not bad. If you are willing to give me that every ninety days, I'll live. And I'll let your friend out of the hole with the first payment. How long do I have to wait?" he asked, smiling.

"Check your account."

"What account?"

"Your bank account!"

"Why would I do that?" he asked suspiciously.

"Just do it." He logged onto the computer and typed in a few keys. Sun-Solé and I both saw his eyes light up.

"What in the . . ."

"Fuck?" I said, finishing his sentence.

"Forty thousand dollars?"

Sun-Solé and I had to do all we could to hold back our laughter. This dude had a hard-on for forty moneybags. My girls and I could wipe our asses with forty before this prison bid happened. But we wanted to make him feel good.

"Yes. Now let Milla out of the hole. Today."

"Done!"

We got up to leave, and his bottom lip was still dangling on the floor. Pink Panther Clique is in the building!

"Girl, did you see the look on his face?" I said to Sun-Solé as we slapped five on our way back to the unit.

"I can't believe we pulled it off. We did it. Made a hit from prison, and we're getting paid. If only I could get home sooner." Then it hit me.

"You can, Sun-Solé. I forgot to tell you. There is a case manager right now taking bribes to give out halfway house time. I bet you if we come correct, we can get you twelve months. Then you'll be out of here six months earlier than you expected."

"Who's taking bribes? How did you find out?"

"Just trust me on this, sis. I know someone who knows someone."

"Okay. Well, I'm down. We can pay whatever the fee is. But for right now, let's just go wait for Milla to get out of the hole. I don't care if we didn't make a penny. This would have all been worth it to save Milla from that charge," I said.

"Most definitely, sis." We were in a good mood. Things were going in our favor. Then suddenly, the smiles were wiped off our faces. The chaplain walked onto the unit, and it got dead quiet. The female chaplain's presence was something like the Grim Reaper. It meant that someone close to one of us on our unit had died.

Please don't let it be me.

Chapter 28

MILLA

It felt so good to walk back on the unit. To be out of the hole. Me and my girls . . . We made it happen. They were waiting for me, and when the door popped, everyone started clapping and cheering! We did it. Even though the odds were stacked against us, we still found a way to be successful. I hugged Eshe and Sun-Solé at the same time. Everybody starting chanting, "Pink Panther, Pink Panther, Pink Panther!" It was dope to hear them shouting for us.

All of the ladies in our unit were able to slice off a piece of the victory pie and eat a little bit for themselves. The guards were standing around, but there was nothing they could do. Our spirits were so high, they could bury us underground, and we'd still feel like we were floating somewhere near the clouds. It felt good.

"All right, settle down so I can give out mail!" the officer stated. Mail call could quiet a room faster than the audience at a Beyoncé concert in less than a second. We didn't play when it came to our mail. He called my name, and I got anxious. I received a letter from King-G, and I couldn't front. I was so happy to hear from him. He had a lot to say:

Jamila,

First and foremost, let me say this. I love you, and I love your drive. Your hard work is not only sexy, but it is helpful. Baby, you just do not know how much your work has kept a brother relevant. I have been fed to the wolves for conspiracy drug charges. And the case against me was so inefficient, had real evidence been required, no jury could ever convict me. But dealing with the Feds, hearsay is all they need to convict. I never realized how dangerous that is. Don't worry, Milla, you are my inspiration to fight this. My family is always going to be associated with the game. It is simply the way I was raised. The life I was born into. I knew nothing else. But as soon as I realized there was a better way, I took a different path.

But our system is so unforgiving to black men. Now, I'll probably spend the rest of my life in prison. All I have is my music and you. I just want to thank you for allowing me to live through my music. This environment is not for the softness. Every day has been a true struggle. When a man is caged like an animal, fed like an animal, or even talked to like an animal, trust, it is not long before he becomes an animal. I am in a battle with myself constantly trying to defeat the beast within me, because alone, I cannot defeat the very beast that has attacked me. My burdensome predator—my own government!

I read his letter over and over again. It touched my heart. How could he say that I was the one keeping him relevant? Not at all. He'd done that for himself. I knew this wasn't the end for him. I was sure that something would give; some law, some new motion or provision would change his circumstances. I folded the letter, and before I could get to my bunk, my name was called again. The officer held out a long yellow envelope. Curiously, I took it from his hand. When I saw the return address, my lips immediately curled into a smile. It was my degree. I completed my course in Religious Studies and had earned my bachelor's degree. I was now on my way to getting my master's. Nothing, and I meant nothing, could stop me.

Eshe and Sun-Solé interrupted my moment. "Girl, who wrote you?" Eshe asked.

"King. And I also got my degree. See!" I said, showing them. They both were just as excited for me as I was for myself. I couldn't wait to get on the phone and tell my parents. They were very supportive and loving. Just when I thought I couldn't get any happier, Eshe and Sun-Solé told me just how much money we made so far.

"Are you kidding me?"

"No. Girl, the song almost has 600,000 downloads now. It's crazy," Sun-Solé said.

"All right! Well, all of us were businesswomen, so let's sit down and kick it about our next move," I said. We found a table on the yard. It would have to do until we were able to sit down at a rectangular marble one on the penthouse floor of our building that we would eventually purchase.

"So check this out. All of this money has to be reinvested. I think we should draw about $20,000 apiece to put on our books, and the rest should get put up," Sun-Solé offered.

"Good idea. But let's not forget about King-G," Eshe added.

"Thank you, sis. I was just gonna take it from my cut, but–"

"Hell, no, Milla! You trippin'! 'Cause I damn sure was gonna give Marcellus and Jerry a cut too."

"You're right, because H will need a cut." Sun-Solé's husband was locked up too, so we all came to an agreement.

"Okay, so let's take about $20,000 and divide it up for our men. It's four of them in total, so that's five apiece. Agreed?"

"Agreed!" we all said in unison.

"Next order of business, I'm leaving soon. I'll be able to get everything pushed up to another level once I hit the bricks," Sun-Solé said. She had the least amount of time among us all. And having a member of our group able to move without restriction would definitely work wonders for us.

"Have they started your halfway house papers?" Milla asked.

"Speaking of that, I think I've got the perfect connect. There is a case manager here. Her name is Ms. Cheiders. Who is your case manager?" Eshe asked.

"Ms. Downing, the young black lady. She's pretty cool."

"Damn, well, that means that Ms. Downing is the one who will request your halfway house papers. We've gotta get Ms. Cheiders to do it," Eshe said.

"But what difference does it make?" I asked.

"Okay, well, check this out. Y'all know white girl Becky?" Everybody nodded. "She put me on to some shit. Ms. Cheiders is taking $20,000 for guaranteed one-year halfway house. She did it for Becky, and that's why she got so much halfway house time."

"What? Girl, you lying!" Sun-Solé said and screwed up her face. But I know her face twisted because she wanted to always be the one to bring the good tea. *Sorry, Sun-Solé, I beat you to it this time,* I thought and chuckled.

"So how do we get this lady to hook up Sun-Solé? And how do we get around the assigned case manager issue? Cheiders would have to have a good excuse for jumping in Ms. Downing's caseload," I added.

"I say we blackmail the bitch. What she's doing is wrong, so why not force her hand by threatening to expose her?"

"You always wanna go the gangster route with shit," Eshe said to Sun-Solé.

"I mean, that seems to be the only thing people respect." Sun-Solé had a point. "Let's talk to the girl Becky." Eshe went inside to find Becky, and we all waited patiently for her to join us.

Becky came outside. Eshe found her in the gym as always. She was dripping sweat. "What's up, guys?" she said.

"Listen, we're just gonna get straight to it. We need the halfway house hookup that we talked about."

"Oh, I, umm, don't know what you're talking about."

"Relax, Becky. These are my girls; they're cool. And we'll even pay you for putting us on. This conversation will not leave this area. I promise," Eshe said.

"Yes, you have all of our word, and our word is bond," I said, touching Becky's hand.

"Okay, well, first and foremost," she said, after calming down, "you'll need $20,000."

"We're good on that. Who do we have to pay? Because I need to get out of here as soon as possible," Sun-Solé said.

"Well, I have to talk to Ms. Cheiders and see how she wants to proceed. It will be a little bit more complicated if you are not on her caseload. But I'm sure we can work something out. I'll talk to her first thing tomorrow."

Becky lived just a few rooms down from me. So, on her way back from visiting with Ms. Cheiders she came to see me.

"So . . .?"

"Here's the deal. She wants to do it. But she's going to talk to Ms. Downing, to try to convince her to allow Sun-Solé to get on her caseload. She's talking to her right now. They're friends. They even car pool to work together, so she'll have no issue, hopefully, getting her to agree. She told me to come back in an hour."

"Okay, if you make this happen, we're going to put an extra $1,000 on your books for the hookup," I said.

"I don't need it."

"That's not the point. It's the way my girls and I do business and show our appreciation. No big deal."

"Well, thank you. I appreciate it. I'll be back after I talk to her." We all went our separate ways.

I waited patiently for Becky to talk to the crooked-ass case manager, and in the meantime, I walked down to Eshe's room. She was in there with Kiera. Eshe didn't usually hang out with anybody other than us, so if Kiera was in her room, Eshe was probably playing savior.

"What's up, girls?" I said as I walked in.

"Hey, Milla! What's up with you?" Eshe said.

"Nothing, just chillin'. I need to talk to you."

"Oh, I can excuse myself," Kiera said.

"Just for a minute," I said, not wanting to be rude. Once Kiera was gone, I had a chance to tell Eshe what was going on, and I explained that I was waiting to hear back from Becky.

"Good. I hope this goes smoothly. Kiera was in here, and I've been talking to her. Ms. Cheiders is her case manager, and after she did over a decade, this woman won't give her more than two months' halfway house. That's foul. I'm trying to help her."

"One thing at a time. We can't help her right now. We gotta focus on Sun-Solé. Our girl is leaving and that takes precedence," I said, reminding Eshe of the order of our priorities.

"Nah, that's not right. There has to be a way to help her. I already gave her my word I would."

"We can't. Not right now. We're doing some real shady shit to get Sun-Solé out early. We can't ruin it by asking too much of the lady. Trust me. I know how you feel. It's unjust. But once we get Sun-Solé's new release date secured, we can help Kiera. You'll just have to push it back a little."

"A'ight, Milla. You got a point. I'll tell Kiera we gotta wait a few weeks." Eshe and I dapped on it. Then I went back to my room to wait on Becky.

A little while later, Becky walked in with a big smile on her face. "Must be good news!" I said, responding to her upbeat mood.

"Absolutely. You're in like Flynn. I told her you had the money and you could make it happen immediately. She said she spoke to Ms. Downing, and she was fine with it. She told her that her and Sun-Solé had a bond already, and she felt it would be easier if she handled her paperwork."

"Really?"

"Yes, and she'll have your people meet her people tomorrow at the RedBarn, the grocery store about five miles from here. She said her person would be parked in a black Malibu in front of the pharmacy. Bring the cash!" And it was done. Our sister was getting out of here earlier, and it was worth every dime.

Chapter 29
SUNNY-SOLÉ

"Why y'all running up in here like Obama got elected for a third term?" I asked Eshe and Milla. They were damn near out of breath.

"Because, bitch, you getting up out of here! The drop goes down in the morning. And we're getting you home to the crib. We got too much we need you to do," Milla responded.

"Stop lying! For real?"

"For real! We were able to pull it off. Ms. Cheiders is so thirsty for money, she'd do anything. You should get your new date soon." We were interrupted by an unexpected guest. Kiera. That's the one thing I hated about cubicles. You couldn't lock your door because there wasn't one.

"So what's going on?" she asked.

"Oh, hey. Whatup, Kiera?" Eshe said.

"What's up?" she said, but I think I sensed a slight attitude. Her neck rolled slightly when she spoke, and her eyes were squinted.

"Everything is good. I'm gonna come and holler at you in a little bit. Let me finish up with my girls, then I'll come down to your room," Eshe explained.

"No, we can talk about this right now. I've been waiting for you since yesterday to come back and tell me how you were gonna figure out how to help me, but you never did. Now I walk in, and I see y'all talking about getting your homegirl out. I thought you were doing this for me first. Isn't that what we talked about?"

No, she didn't come up in here trying to check Eshe. She had one more thing to say before I went off.

"Hold up! Let me be clear," Eshe said. "I know you don't think you're comin' up in here checkin' me, boo. I promised you I would help, and I will. But I have to handle somethin' first. I got you. But you need to chill out with all that."

"Nah, I'm just sayin'. Y'all walk around here like your shit don't stink and doin' all this extra shit, but for real, you just blew hot smoke up my ass. If you didn't plan on helping me, then why not just say so? I've done over a decade. I can handle whatever. You a baby in the prison game, but you think you a vet."

Now the bitch was getting on *my* nerves. I stood up and approached her before Eshe could even respond.

"Yo, get the fuck out my room, ma. You doing too much right now with all that disrespectful shit."

"I was leaving anyway," she said, throwing up her hand and walking out.

"People got a lot of shit with them for real. How she gon' come up in here talking crazy? You're doing her a favor."

"It's all good. She's just upset with the system. Not us. I'll deal with her later. In the meantime, let's make sure that the drop goes right today." Eshe got right back to business like the bullshit never even happened. That's what I respected about her. She didn't give things that weren't deserving of her attention any play.

"I'm so anxious. I hope this goes well. Look at my hands, they're shaking. This is major right here. Paying for halfway house. Who would have ever thought? Yo, we've gotta do something to kill the time," I said.

"Here we go with your eye-spy Molly Maid shit. Where do you wanna go now?" Milla asked. She knew me well. I had the perfect thing for us to do to entertain ourselves while we waited to make sure the drop went well.

"You know today Prego's husband is coming to see her. I wanna be down there to see that shit. I got permission for us to go and clean up visitation. It's something to do to calm my nerves."

Mayhem struck the visiting room. Lieutenant Longwood and Prego's husband fought. It was crazy. "I knew going down there was a bad idea," Milla said.

"No, it wasn't. Now we know who her baby father is for real. Now, *that* is some scandalous shit. I can't believe she lost her baby due to miscarriage, never told her husband, then turned around and got pregnant by the lieutenant. Now, *that* is some shit right there," I said, thinking about the whole situation out loud.

"Well . . . That's not *really* what happened," Eshe said.

"What do you mean that's not what happened? We all saw it and heard it with our own eyes."

"Sun-Solé, you already know. In prison, we believe only half of what we see and almost none of what we hear. On the way out, she told me something. And I just couldn't believe it," Eshe said.

"What? Tell us." I needed to know what was going on around here. That is what kept me calm, knowing what was happening in this deranged prison world is what kept me feeling like I had a grip on things. Even if it was just a façade; it felt good. It was just one less piece of control they had.

"Okay. Well, when they were separating us from helping Prego, she told me that Lieutenant Longwood is not the father!"

"What? Wait. So that means the husband really is . . .? That doesn't make any sense. She would be almost a year pregnant! Impossible," I said, doing the math in my head.

"Nope, the husband isn't either. It's the warden," Eshe whispered.

"The *warden?* You lying, girl!" I said, shaking my head.

"Nope. Turns out she's been fucking him too, the entire time. And Longwood has no idea." I couldn't believe it. And here I was thinking he liked me.

"Fix your face, Sun-Solé," Milla said, laughing. "So what? Your prison boyfriend got somebody pregnant. You're married."

"Shut up, girl. There is nothing wrong with my face. I'm just shocked."

"Well, I just hope you didn't do nothing with him too. *Did* you?" Milla asked.

"And if she did? So what if she did. It's not a big deal."

"What do you mean 'no big deal'? Of course, it would be a big deal. She's married."

"Oh, I forgot. I'm talking to a preacher."

"Whatever!" Milla said.

"First of all, I'm just saying. If she wanted to handle her business to further the cause, we can't judge her. That's all I'm saying. You don't think if H could get out tomorrow by banging his case manager, he wouldn't?" Eshe said.

"Girl, you know how men are. He probably would," I confirmed. I was no fool. H and I had our share of marital issues like all couples. But it was never anything big enough to tear us apart. When you dealt with a king, females always tried your hand. It didn't matter, though. He always proved his loyalty was to me. And our tribulations just made our love that much stronger. "Look, I love my husband, and I had no intentions on getting busy with the warden. I'm just surprised, that's all. This is crazy. If this ever gets out . . . boy, oh boy."

"Well, whatever. It's not our problem. We got bigger things to worry about. The drop should have happened by now. So let's call your people, Sun-Solé, and see how it went," Milla said, changing the subject. The three of us walked to the payphones and waited for her to make the call. She hung up in two minutes. Then she sank down to the floor.

"What? What's wrong?" Eshe asked me.

"No good! He said no good! When he got to the supermarket, there were already police there. Everywhere. And they had the black Malibu surrounded. My guy left just in time, but something still went down." The feeling in my stomach was hard to explain. It felt like I was going down a roller coaster, and the tracks just snapped. Impending disaster!

It didn't take long for us to figure out what happened. Prison news traveled just as fast as news on the outside—if not faster, in some cases. The warden, assistant warden, captain, and lieutenants came on to our unit and ordered an emergency lockdown. A man in a suit, undeniably an FBI agent, walked straight over to Kiera's room, and they escorted her out.

Turns out that we made an enemy. Kiera! Kiera went to Ms. Cheiders and told her that she would turn us all in if she didn't get her due halfway house. She told her she knew about her taking bribes. Ms. Cheiders, being the slick bitch she is, told Ms. Downing that she was swamped and needed her to pick up a package from a friend at the supermarket. And she told her she could use her car. It was no big deal since they car pooled anyway.

On her lunch break, Downing went to the supermarket just like her friend asked her to. She cluelessly accepted the package, but it was from an undercover. As soon as she got back in the car, the Feds surrounded her. She was arrested for accepting the money. When everything finally got ironed out, Cheiders blamed the whole scandal on Downing. Of course, they believed it. Why not? Cheiders was white. Downing was black.

It was horrible, and all three of us felt like shit. An innocent woman went down. None of this would have happened if it wasn't for the corruption in the system to begin with. It was ripe for exploitation, and Cheiders was just one of many who played on the needs of inmates to get back to their families. The entire setup was criminal in and of itself.

Chapter 30

ESHE

After every inmate who ever dealt with Ms. Downing had been questioned over and over for months, she got hit with five years. Ain't that some shit? Even though she was innocent. I'm sure it shook other staff members to the core. At the end of the day, it was easy to go from wearing blue to green. Or blue to khaki. Becoming an inmate was just as easy as it was to become a widow or a person in debt. It could happen to anyone. So it was important to treat others the way you wanted to be treated because you just never know what might happen.

The count had just cleared, and they called us to get mail. Ever since our song dropped, they had to bring up a separate mailbag just for the Pink Panther Clique. Our song was bringing attention to the injustices that took place in prison. People were paying attention, wondering who these chicks were that were locked up. Did they really deserve all that time? When my name was called, I went up and grabbed my mail. I could recognize those typed letters from anywhere:

UNITED STATES FEDERAL COURT

221 CADMAN PLAZA

BROOKLYN, NEW YORK

I didn't know what to expect. When I opened the letter, it said that I had another hearing for the murder charge. I tried to push that reality to the back of my mind throughout my bid. I figured that if I didn't think about it, it would somehow go away. But that's not how it worked. I had to be in court in just eight days. That meant that I was going on a trip.

"Milla, this stuff is for you to hold. And Sun-Solé, put all these clothes up, please."

"What? You got immediate release or something?" Sun-Solé asked.

"Nah. Not at all. I wish. I never talked to you guys in detail about it, because I try not to think about it, but you know I got that pending murder charge of a United States Secret Service agent. I didn't do it and neither did my team. My bros are all my codefendants in the case. But here's the deal . . . If it looks like they are going to charge Jerry or Marcellus, I'm going to take the rap for it."

"Girl, hell, no! Are you crazy?"

"Nah, just loyal. It's my ship, and they were trying to set me up, not them. So I would never let them go down for something I did if I can help it."

"That's noble and all, Eshe, but at the end of the day, husbands have tried to save wives, mothers have tried to take the hit for sons, but it doesn't matter. The Feds don't work that way. Once they've got their eyes on you, it doesn't matter what anybody else says. You'll just have to fight. Good luck, sis. We'll hold your property for you."

What Milla told me was true. She was right. The Feds had their eyes on pinning this murder on all of us, and that is exactly what they would try to do. Two days later, I was told to pack out my belongings. I was going on a writ to court. A writ simply meant that another court had demanded my presence. It was cool, and I figured that I would get picked up by the marshals. But that's not what happened. I was catching a plane ride. On the lovely, most coveted airlines: CON-AIR!

I was taken down to R&D, where I was stripped out and told to change into blue skips, superloose fitting khakis, and last but not least, I had to remove all of my pride. I'd never been on Con-Air before, but I heard horror stories about it. Once I was good and shackled from waist to ankles, they were ready to drive me to the airport. It was a sight I'd never seen before. There were about twenty Greyhound-sized buses, full of men. Thousands of men, it seemed. A large plane was sitting far off at the airport, and all these buses surrounded the plane, leaving only enough space for the airplane to back out. I was told to step out of the van. The cold breeze made the iron and chains around my body feel like knives. The weight of the cold metal on my ankles stung.

"Remove your shoes one at a time!" a female marshal said to me. I had to somehow maneuver my foot out of my shoe while shackled. The woman felt the inside of my shoe thoroughly. She then felt my socks and tossed my shoe back on the ground. She repeated the same act, and then told me to turn around and look at the ground. It was so humiliating. I could feel that I was being watched, but I didn't want to turn around. Six armed men carrying assault rifles surrounded the area as well.

"If you move the wrong way, look the wrong way, or even think to get out of line, one of these air marshals *will* shoot. And when I say shoot, I do mean shoot—to kill. So remain quiet and follow our orders. Do you understand?"

There were a few "yes sirs" from some of the bitch-ass men that were scared of these clowns. But I remained stoic. I refused to give in to the slave masters. I happened to look up, and a man standing directly across from me caught my eye. I knew I wasn't supposed to look at him, but I couldn't help myself. His beauty was captivating. His long dreads were pulled back into a ponytail, and his goatee was perfectly lined up. The white, government-issued T-shirt barely fit him. His muscles protruded through his shirt, and he was covered in tattoos. *Fine* was an understatement. I stared at him, and when I caught myself, the marshal caught me too.

"Is there something about what I said that you didn't understand? I thought I made myself clear earlier. Do not look at the men. That's an order. Try me again and you'll be wearing a box, you understand?" he asked, screaming in my ear. I looked back down at the ground. "Oh, so you're deaf?" he asked. Then he looked at the other marshal. "We got us a deaf one over here. Maybe she needs some *special* attention!" What the fuck did that mean? I didn't move. I heard more footsteps coming up behind me.

"You must not speak English, Aisha Haller. You think you're special?" I hadn't even done anything. Why were they fucking with me? I could see them loading people onto the plane. I just wanted to get to my destination and get away from these people. "Hello!" the marshal said, angry that I was ignoring him.

"Ay, yo! Why don't you back up from the lady? Y'all some real bitch-ass muh'fuckas to be picking on a girl." I looked up, and the guy with the dreads was speaking up for me. I couldn't believe his boldness. It immediately made some private places throb. All the attention was now on him. I was told to get on the plane, but I was concerned about him. What were they going to do to him? Just that fast, there were ten marshals all up in his grill. I was pushed up the steps and told to sit in the fourth row. The first three rows were reserved for BOP officials and Air Marshals.

I was able to get a window seat. There were hundreds of men out there. A sea of them being carted and hauled like brown parcels. I searched for him. And I saw him standing his ground as they put the black box on him and tightened his cuffs. It didn't seem to faze him as they led him to the plane. A minute later, he was walking past me. I could smell the testosterone leaking from his pores. He was all man. When he walked past me, he winked. I smiled, not caring about their rules. He was taken to the back of the plane and a marshal sat next to him.

After takeoff, I had to use the bathroom. The bathroom was in the back, and I knew I would have to walk past him. That was really my true motivation for saying I had to pee.

He mouthed his number to me. His federal identification. The last three numbers were 037, which meant he was from Baltimore. I nodded and mouthed the words, "thank you," letting him know I'd gotten his number, and I'd also appreciated him standing up for me to the bullies. He was fearless, and his boldness was obvious. His actions seemed to say: *nothing they could do would ever faze me.*

By the time I got to court, my lawyer was already waiting for me. He came to see me in the bull pen, and he advised me to take the plea. They were offering ten years on a conspiracy to murder charge. I didn't want to take it, but when he told me the alternative, I knew I had to really think about this. "And what about my brothers? What are they offering them?"

"Don't worry about them. You need to worry about yourself. It's my job as your attorney to advise you as such. And their lawyers will be advising them of the same."

"Well, that part of your advice is not necessary. Would you abandon your family in a crisis just because it would warrant the best result for you?" He didn't answer. "My point exactly. So like I said, what's up with my brothers?"

"I think you all have been offered the same. I'll see you inside. They're ready for us." He left the bull pen, and I was escorted to the courtroom.

The judge walked in, of course, expressionless. But it was a great day because a few minutes later, my brothers Marcellus and Jerry entered the courtroom and stood beside me with their lawyers. I reached out my hands to them. I embraced them both and told them how much I loved them and thanked them for being down. But all of that only happened in my mind. I just hoped they were temporarily telepathic, and they could feel what I was feeling inside. Their loyalty was true, and I respected them for it enormously.

"Have you all decided to proceed to trial? From what I've been told, there have been three plea offers. Counsel, have any of your clients agreed?" the judge asked.

"No, Your Honor. We're still in negotiation," my attorney said.

"Well, let me make it simple for you. The pleas offered are ten years apiece. It's obvious you all are not going to testify against one another. Let's make this easy. Thirty years is the combined jail time. I don't care how you split it up, but I will not go below that amount of time. Not for the death of an agent. An American hero." I wanted to tell him to shut up. This was so unprofessional. Without any proof, without hearing testimony, or even knowing for sure if there will be a trial, he already pegged us as guilty. This wasn't justice. This so-called American hero was falsely setting me up, planting drugs in my office. And drugs were chosen because as a black successful company, it would be easy to convince a jury that drugs are the real way we made our money. Not through brains, wit, intelligence, and strategic planning to run a corporation. Only street shit. And that was the insult. As I thought about it, I made up my mind.

I tapped my lawyer. "Not now!" he whispered.

"Tell him to set a trial date!"

"No, you'll lose."

"Just set the date!"

"Excuse me, Your Honor, my client, Aisha Haller, has just informed me that she'd like to continue her plea of not guilty, and proceed to trial."

"My client has just informed me of the same," Jerry's lawyer said.

"Mine as well, Your Honor!" Marcellus's attorney spoke up. We all nodded at each other. We were sticking together and hoping for the best.

"Okay, trial is set for six months from now. This court is adjourned!"

Epilogue

Eshe and Milla wiped the tears from their faces, only to have to wipe them again. Sun-Solé was leaving. She completed the drug program, which took twelve months off her sentence. Plus, she got a year halfway house. The program was the only way to get out of federal prison early without snitching. So she was on her way to the crib. Her son was in pre-k, and he'd been waiting for her for a while. They knew all of this, but her absence still hurt. They had formed a bond that only people who did time together would understand.

Nevertheless, Eshe and Milla still had many years to do. There were advantages to having their partner in the street, but they just couldn't feel it yet. Their bond was too strong, and it felt like they were losing a piece of themselves. When a friend went home from prison, it was one of the most bittersweet moments a person could experience. Of course, you wanted them to be free, but the longing for their companionship was still intense.

It had been a week since Sun-Solé left, and Eshe and Milla were strategizing their next move. They had plenty of money now, but that didn't matter. They still prisoners and could only spend $360 a month, no matter what. Their financial status didn't catapult them to any levels above anyone else. That is one thing prison did: it placed everyone on the same level, regardless of who you were or where you came from. They still wore a prisoner's uniform every day, and they were still counted like cattle like everybody else. They quickly learned that, in reality, money was only a small part of freedom. A very small part at that. True freedom came from allowing yourself to be free in the mind. And that was not an easy thing when your environment reflected concrete walls and blue-clad officers telling you when you could and couldn't breathe. It was degrading. And with Sun-Solé gone, the feeling of loneliness set in for a while.

Some months later, Eshe found out about the dude she'd met during her Con-Air adventure. She had someone look up his number. Jessie Haller. Coincidentally, they had the same last name. "Yo, Eshe, that's fate!" Milla said. "I'm telling you. What are the odds of that? It's God! Jesus!"

"Girl, bye! I better make sure he's not my damn cousin."

"If so, he's probably like your tenth cousin or so, so it won't matter," she joked. They laughed. And Milla encouraged Eshe to write him. She finally did, and it would turn out to be one of the most important decisions of her life.

As far as the drama in their prison went, Prego wasn't pregnant anymore, but that name had stuck to her like the word *felon* stuck to a prisoner's life story. That's still what everyone called her. All the ladies, however, felt bad for her. With so many mothers locked up together, even with beefs and disagreements, at the end of the day, there was a level of connection among all the ladies there. The permanent state of Prego's depression infected the unit like a disease. Seeing her was a sad reminder of how helpless an inmate truly was. She gave birth more than six months ago, but she still hadn't seen her son. She still had some time to do, and her husband had taken the baby, refusing to let her see him. He knew the child did not belong to him, but he did not care. He was her husband, so legally, that baby was his.

Lieutenant Longwood quit that fateful day when the fight broke out. But he'd only done so because he planned to have a life with Prego. Once he realized there was a chance that the baby might not be his, he tried to get his job back. He was lucky that he didn't get arrested. But since he'd already resigned and that was his last day anyway, the BOP didn't do anything. And that turned out to be a grave mistake.

It was early in the morning, the inmate population was locked down for staff appreciation day. Longwood was young, only thirty-eight, but he started with the BOP at the tender age of eighteen. Before he quit, he had almost twenty full years in. They set up for the day as if it was a real holiday. The inmates could see the entire event from the window in the recreation hall. With nothing else to do, many of them pulled up a seat and watched the officers have a block party fully paid for by the American taxpayers' hard-earned money.

"Hey, Milla!" Eshe screamed out. "Come here and look!"

"I don't wanna see none of those clowns."

"Yeah, but you might want to see this one!"

Milla walked over to look out of the window and couldn't believe what she was seeing.

"Is that . . ."

"Longwood? Yeah, it looks that way!" He was wearing a black hoodie, standing off to the far right corner by himself. He didn't look like he was going to join in and participate in any of the festivities. All eyes were on him because so many rumors had circulated about him after he quit. Staff could often be overheard talking about how he routinely came back up to the prison begging for his job back. He was pissed that he changed his life for a woman who was fucking his boss.

Someone went and got Prego and brought her to the window as well so she could see her angry-looking ex-boyfriend crashing the party. Because of all his time with the bureau, he was able to get in without too much scrutiny. All of the officers were laughing and joking and enjoying the day.

The warden was in the clear. Prego had some sick love for him, and she never told on him. In reality, any time an officer has sex with an inmate, it is automatically rape, due to the vulnerability of the inmate. He was able to keep his job. He joined the party, and when he walked out onto the floor, his staff clapped for him. All but Lieutenant Longwood, that is.

"Oh no!" Milla said. "Look, he's got a gun!" Longwood crept up toward the unsuspecting warden and pointed his gun. All of the women screamed, but they were behind glass, and nobody could hear them. They were banging, trying to warn him, but they were the nobodies of the world, and not a soul acknowledged their faces staring down onto the private courtyard reserved for staff and inmate weddings. Their warnings were ignored.

POP! POP!

Two loud gunshots sounded, and all of the staff members took off running.

POP! POP! POP!

Three more shots and the warden went down. The ladies screamed. Longwood seemed to be moving in slow motion. He looked up, straight at the windows to the unit and looked Prego dead in the eyes. The menacing look was enough to scare any sane person. Then he looked in the direction of the door. The emergency exit door that led to the unit, and he took off running toward it.

"Oh my God! Everybody hide! He's coming!"

About the Author

 Aisha Hall, also known as A. Rochester, was born and raised in Roosevelt, New York. Her love for writing stories and music started as a child. She developed leadership skills at a very young age and was eager to put those skills to the test. This led to her falling in love with the idea of using her creative mind to make a living.

For a while, Aisha found her success, but at the age of twenty-five, she caught a federal conspiracy charge, sending her to prison to serve a sentence of more than ten years! It wasn't until her incarceration that she decided to write her first novel. She refused to let her circumstances hold her back. Aisha has become an activist, bringing awareness to the epidemic of women and mass incarceration. She also encourages all people who are imprisoned to use that time to better themselves and focus on their future. Aisha believes that when you are pursuing your dreams, the Universe will assist you in ways that are sometimes disguised as failure. "Never give up or give in; just go hard!" is her motto.

About the Author

Jamila T. Davis, born and raised in Jamaica, Queens, New York, is a motivational speaker, prison reform activist, and the author of several books geared to inspire and empower readers to overcome adversity. Davis is no stranger to triumphs and defeats. By the age of twenty-five, she utilized her business savvy and street smarts to rise to the top of her field, becoming a lead go-to person in the hip-hop music industry and a self-made millionaire through real estate investments. All seemed well . . . until Davis's empire suddenly crumbled. She was convicted of bank fraud for her role in a multimillion-dollar bank fraud scheme and sentenced to twelve-and-a-half years in federal prison. Behind bars, Davis used her time to discover her gifts and talents and began her plight to advocate for change within the U.S judicial system. While incarcerated, she became a bestselling author, cofounded a nonprofit organization, obtained multiple college degrees, and assisted in creating several films.

About the Author

Sunshine Smith-Williams is a serial entrepreneur, philanthropist, mentor, motivational speaker, and author. Raised in Jamaica, Queens, New York, by a single mother who struggled to make ends meet, Smith-Williams grew up in multiple impoverished housing projects with dim hopes. Utilizing education as a weapon to overcome poverty, she obtained several degrees and certifications, climbing the corporate ladder to achieve success.

After being laid off from her dream job in 2010, Smith-Williams gained the faith to start her own consultant firm, "Sunny Legal Realty LLC." Through an intense journey, she discovered—and dethroned—her flaws and increased her self-esteem. As a result, she successfully opened several thriving businesses and mentored others to do the same.

In May 2013, Smith-Williams made a poor choice and reunited with an old friend and gave him a ride that eventually cost her, her freedom. This experience enlightened Smith-Williamson to her purpose. Her life is a living testament that the past, regardless of the mistakes you make or your background, does not have to dictate your future!

Life after prison stopped nothing for the young entrepreneur. This past year, the African American Film Critic Association named her self-help book, *Sunny 101: The 10 Commandments of a Boss Chick,* an honorable mention among the top ten books of 2015.

In spring 2016, Smith-Williams was honored for change by the Board of Education and has done motivational speaking throughout the state of New York. She shares this message of hope with both youth and adults, inspiring them to overcome life's difficulties.

Currently, Smith-Williams resides in a suburb in Nassau County, New York, with her husband (business partner) and their eight-year-old son.

From Inmate to the *New York Times* Best seller.

Three-time *New York Times* bestselling author Wahida Clark has become one of the most sought after Urban Lit authors of this generation and is one of only 4 Urban Lit authors to appear on the *New York Times* bestseller list.

Wahida Clark has an amazing story. Tenacity, vision and sheer determination are what brought her to where she is today.

Clark began writing her first novel while serving a 9 ½ year prison sentence, including 9 months in solitary confinement, at the Lexington Prison Camp in Lexington, Ky.While behind bars, Clarkinked a publishing deal with a major publishing house, wrote *and* released 7 novels and laid the groundwork for her publishing company, Wahida Clark Presents Publishing.

To date she has released 14 successful novels including THREE *New York Times* bestsellers. Her own publishing company, Wahida Clark Presents is one of the fastest growing independent publishing houses in the country. In just 4 short years, WCP has earned nearly 1 million dollars in sales, has 26 titles currently in stores across the country and has a roster of 25 established urban authors.

Reading Group Discussion Questions
Pink Panther Clique

1) Of the three women, Milla, Eshe, and Sun-Solé, which of them received the most unjust sentence?

2) Why was Milla's boss okay with her bending the rules? How often do you think that happens in corporate America?

3) If Prego's relationship with Lieutenant Longwood was consensual, do you think it is right that it's automatically considered rape?

4) Do you think Eshe and her team will eventually be convicted of murder?

5) Why was Eshe's business considered such a threat to corporate America?

6) Do you think that King-G, Milla's boyfriend, deserved to go to prison? If so, was he deserving of a life sentence?

7) Why do you think the Pink Panther Clique's music did so well?

8) Do you think it will come out that Sun-Solé messed around with the warden as well?

9) Why do you think there is there so much corruption in this prison? And should the girls have exposed it first, or were they right to exploit the corruption and use it for their

benefit?

10) What do you think is going to happen once Lieutenant Longwood gets into the women's housing unit with his gun?

Other Books by Aisha Hall:

Keema and Lamar: A Ghetto Love Story (Book Series 1–3)
Caught Up Loving a Boss
The Swipe Life (By Shawana King with Aisha Hall)
The Backside of the Story (By Kimberly Smedley with A. Rochester)

Other Books by Jamila Davis:

She's All Caught Up!
The High Price I Had to Pay (Book Series 1–3)
Voices of Consequences Enrichment Series (Book Series 1–3)

Other Books by Sunshine Smith-Williams:

The 10 Commandments of a Boss Chick
Broken Pencils Still Write

Other Books by Wahida Clark

Thugs and The Women Who Love Them
Every Thug Needs A Lady
Thug Matrimony
Thug Lovin'
Justify My Thug
Honor Thy Thug
Thugs: Seven
Payback is A Mutha
The Golden Hustla

CPSIA information can be obtained
at www.ICGtesting.com
Printed in the USA
JSHW050354010322
R11473400001B/R114734PG23318JSX00001B/1